You don't *have* to read the Hi⟨ **P9-CES-582**
But if you want to, this is the right order:

Book 1: How to Train Your Dragon
Book 2: How to Be a Pirate
Book 3: How to Speak Dragonese
Book 4: How to Cheat a Dragon's Curse
Book 5: How to Twist a Dragon's Tale
Book 6: A Hero's Guide to Deadly Dragons
Book 7: How to Ride a Dragon's Storm
Book 8: How to Break a Dragon's Heart
Book 9: How to Steal a Dragon's Sword
Book 10: How to Seize a Dragon's Jewel
Book 11: How to Betray a Dragon's Hero

# WARNING

Any relationship to any historical fact WHATSOEVER is entirely coincidental.

## YOU HAVE BEEN WARNED

## ABOUT HICCUP

Hiccup Horrendous Haddock the Third was
an awesome swordfighter, a dragon whisperer,
and the greatest Viking Hero who ever lived.
But Hiccup's memoirs look back to when
he was a very ordinary boy who found
it hard to be a Hero.

Hiccup Horrendous Haddock the Third.
Toothless and Wodensfang
Stoick the Vast
Stormfly
Fishlegs
Camicazi

*This book is dedicated to JOHNNIE WILLIS-BUND with love from his god mother*

Text and illustrations copyright © 2013 by Cressida Cowell

Little, Brown and Company

Hachette Book Group
237 Park Avenue, New York, NY 10017
Visit our website at lb-kids.com

Little, Brown and Company is a division of Hachette Book Group, Inc.
The Little, Brown name and logo are trademarks of Hachette Book Group, Inc.

The publisher is not responsible for websites (or their content) that are not owned by the publisher.

First U.S. Trade Paperback Edition: September 2014
First U.S. Hardcover Edition: December 2013
Originally published in Great Britain in 2013 by Hodder Children's Books

Library of Congress Cataloging-in-Publication Data

Cowell, Cressida.
  How to betray a dragon's hero / by Cressida Cowell. — First U.S. edition.
    pages cm. — (How to train your dragon ; book 11)
  Summary: "Hiccup is in hiding in the Murderous Mountains with the Company of the Dragonmark, but he is determined to become King of the Wilderwest by defeating the witch's Vampire Spydragons and steal back the King's Things from Alvin the Treacherous"—Provided by publisher.
  ISBN 978-0-316-24412-1 (hc)— ISBN 978-0-316-24411-4 (pb)
  1. Vikings—Juvenile fiction. [1. Vikings—Fiction. 2. Dragons—Fiction.] I. Title.
  PZ7.C83535Hld 2013
  [Fic] —dc23
                      2013027456

10 9 8 7 6 5 4 3 2 1

RRD-C

Printed in the United States of America

*Simon Cowell, Anne McNeil, Naomi Potterman, Jennifer Stephenson, and Judit Komar, for all their help in the making of this book.*

# How to Betray a Dragon's Hero

## by Cressida Cowell

## LITTLE, BROWN AND COMPANY
New York   Boston

Dragonmarker ships
MURDE
ROU
Waterfall
Coral Beach
WRECKER'S BAY
Hero's End
SINGING SANDS OF THE FERRYMAN'S GIFT
THE REEF
Hero's Gap
ISLAND of TOMORROW

Alvinsmen ships
THE TREE HIDEOUT
LANDS
THE WINTER WIND OF WODEN

# ~ CONTENTS ~

# The Cursed Island of Tomorrow

We have not yet seen Tomorrow. We have not yet dared go there.

There was once a thriving city on the island of Tomorrow. The flags of the Wilderwest flew bravely from the towers of its hundred splendid castles. It was a city built on the enslavement of men and of dragons, but, like many a city before and after it, it was a handsome and glorious city nonetheless.

But a century ago, Grimbeard the Ghastly, the Last King of the Wilderwest, did a truly dreadful thing.

Grimbeard's son Hiccup Horrendous Haddock the Second, with his dragon Furious, was leading a peaceful dragon petition to plead with his father to end the misery of slavery. Grimbeard mistook the petition for rebellion. He killed his very own son by his very own sword, the Stormblade, and the blood of his son was spilled on the seat of his very own Throne.

That was the beginning of the curse upon the Throne and the island of Tomorrow. The city was destroyed by the dragon forces that had come at first in peaceful protest. The hundred splendid castles were burned to the ground, and the dragon Furious was captured and bound in inescapable chains, in the depths of a forest prison.

Grimbeard the Ghastly repented of his terrible crime. He swore that there would never be a King of the Wilderwest again, unless that King could be a better man than he was. So Grimbeard created an Impossible Task. He scattered ten of the King's Things in all four corners of the distant earth.

Those things would be guarded by monsters and dragons most terrible. Only a true Hero could gather the things together and lift the curse and become the next King of the Wilderwest.

In the unlikely event that there would ever be a Hero great enough to gather those ten Lost Things, the Hero could then be crowned, but only on the twelfth day of Doomsday, known as the Doomsday of Yule, which comes but once a year, and only on the island of Tomorrow, on the stumps of the Throne where Grimbeard's son had died.

In the meantime, Grimbeard appointed human and dragon Warriors to be Guardians on the ruined island fortress of Tomorrow, so fearsome and so terrible that they can barely be imagined. All will kill on sight anyone illegally entering their territory.

Now the Archipelago needs a King more than ever before, for the dragon Furious has escaped from that forest prison where Grimbeard the Ghastly once enslaved him, and the dragon is carrying out his own curse on the humans whom he now hates. His intention is to extinguish the entire human race.

And the dragon Furious is winning. He has torched the whole north of the Archipelago. The humans have been forced to live in hiding places underground for fear of the dragon.

Nothing can stop the dragon Furious now. Nothing except for a new King, for a new King will be told the Secret of the tenth Lost Thing, the Dragon Jewel, a jewel that has the power to destroy dragons forever.

There is only one time in the year that a possible King is allowed to enter the territory of Tomorrow.

It is on one of the twelve mornings of the twelve days of Doomsday.

Today it is midwinter, and the morning of the ninth day of Doomsday.

Here he is now, the extraordinarily tall figure of a lone Ferryman, rowing from the dreadful island of Tomorrow, across the little causeway of Hero's Gap, to the mainland of the Murderous Mountains.

The Ferryman is the Druid Guardian of the island of Tomorrow. He is blindfolded and cannot take off this blindfold until a new King of the Wilderwest is crowned. The blindfold signifies his role as an impartial and implacable judge, and his absolute commitment to his role as a Druid Guardian. But by some supernatural agency, he seems able to sense that there is a figure, with a little band of followers, waiting for him on the beach. The figure is UG the Uglithug. His hope rises.

At last…in the nick of time…a Hero, come to claim the Kingdom!

For the Druid Guardian fears that the dragon Furious is very close to extinguishing the human race.

The Druid Guardian brings the boat to a sludgy halt on the beach known as the Singing Sands of the Ferryman's Gift and spreads wide his arms and makes the declaration, as his father, and his father's father, and his father's father's father have done every year before him.

"He-or-she-who-would-be-king, approach Tomorrow if you dare! Only the one with the King's Lost Things can be crowned the King and live…"

And then he turns to UG the Uglithug and asks these solemn words.

"Are you he-who-would-be-king?"

UG replies, "I am."

"Are you the chosen representative of all the Tribes of the Archipelago?" asks the Druid Guardian.

UG nods.

"Have you brought a gift for the Ferryman?" asks the Druid Guardian.

"I have," replies UG the Uglithug.

The Druid Guardian says solemnly, but with eager hope, "Then show me the things."

UG the Uglithug snaps his fingers to his followers, and one by one they bring forward the things.

They are: a fang-free dragon, Grimbeard's second-best sword, the Roman shield, an arrow-from-the-land-that-does-not-exist, the heart's stone, the ticking-thing, the key-that-opens-all-locks, the Throne, the Crown, the Dragon Jewel.

UG the Uglithug's followers lay them out on the beach before the Druid Guardian and retreat. The Druid Guardian steps forward to examine the things.

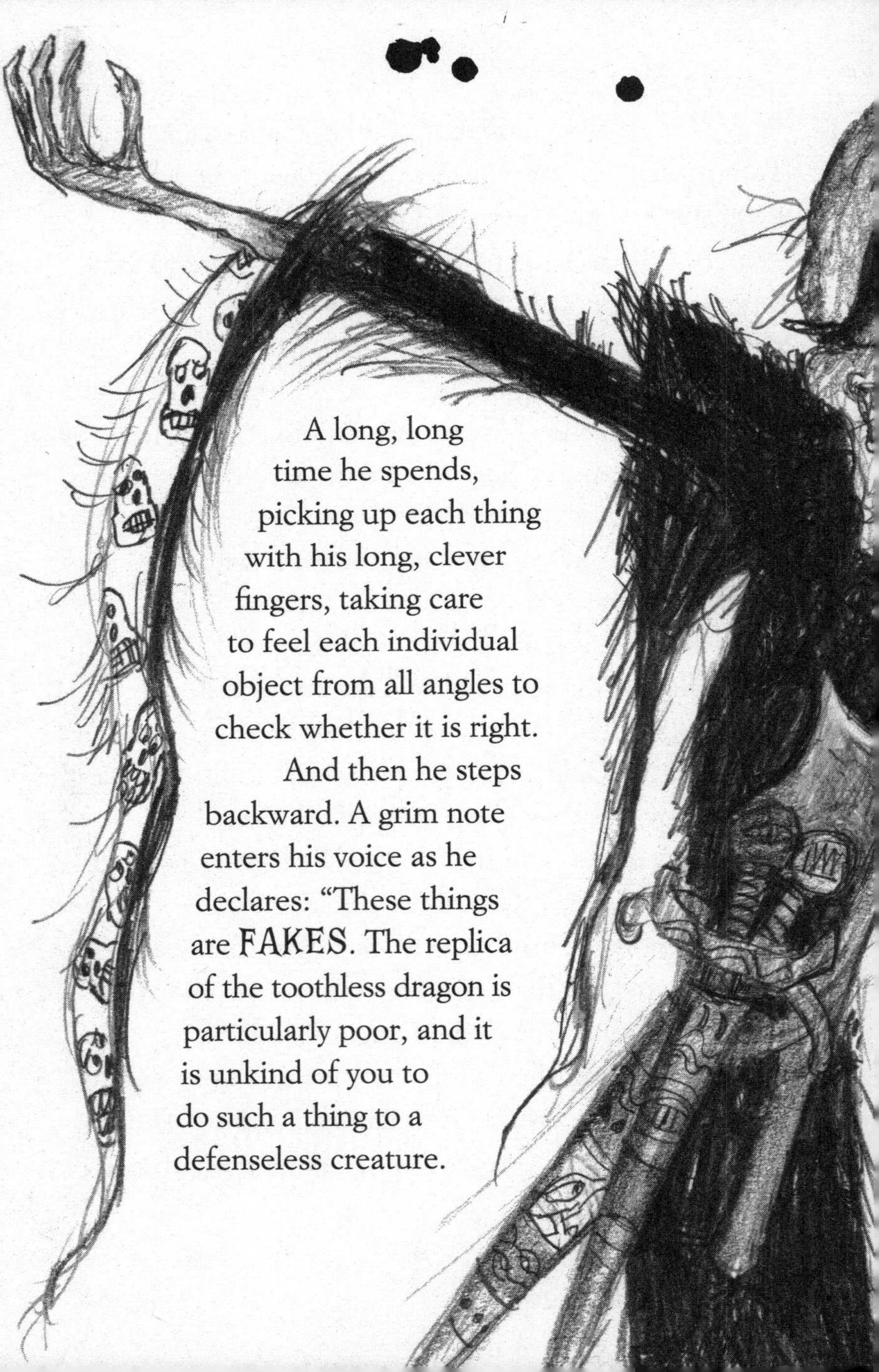

A long, long
time he spends,
picking up each thing
with his long, clever
fingers, taking care
to feel each individual
object from all angles to
check whether it is right.
And then he steps
backward. A grim note
enters his voice as he
declares: "These things
are FAKES. The replica
of the toothless dragon is
particularly poor, and it
is unkind of you to
do such a thing to a
defenseless creature.

We will give it
a home on Tomorrow."
(UG the Uglithug has
removed the teeth from a poor
little Trotterdragon in order
to pretend it is the real toothless
dragon from the prophecy.)

UG the Uglithug turns as white
as a sheep's fleece. "As for YOU, UG
the Uglithug," continues the Druid
Guardian, "know this. He who dares
to approach Tomorrow with a gift
that is unacceptable dies a quick and
horrible death along with his followers.
"ARISE, YOU GUARDIAN
PROTECTORS OF TOMORROW!
ARISE AND DO YOUR WORST!"

All around UG the Uglithug and his followers on the beach, the sand begins to bubble. And then the land gives birth to creatures of unimaginable horror, huge and terrible, screaming vengeance. There is no time for reaction, no time for defense. UG the Uglithug and his followers have no time to see even what they are, whether they are dragons or something worse.

These creatures take hold of UG the Uglithug.

They take hold of

the followers, screaming and struggling. They shoot upward and ever upward, up into the sky, up and up and up, into the clouds beyond, into the choking freeze of ice and fire of the upper atmosphere, and those people are then no more. They will return to the earth only as ash and purple rain.

Such is the vengeance of the Guardians of Tomorrow on those who try to approach their shore without the correct things.

The Druid Guardian sighs. He gently caresses the head of the poor toothless Trotterdragon, reassuring it softly that all will be well. He mutters to himself, "Three more days...only three more days for a Hero to arrive and save us all."

Wearily, he clambers back into his little boat. He is not really expecting that right Hero to come, you see. Why would he? This is a ritual that has taken place every year for ninety-nine years, and only the unworthy have come. Wearily, the old man begins to row back to Tomorrow.

He will call for a Hero to come and claim the crown for three more days. If a Hero does not arrive on the eleventh day, on Doomsday Eve, then it will be too late. Grimbeard's rules, set down a century ago, are inviolate. The borders of Tomorrow will close again until the following year.

And next year really WILL be too late. By then the dragon Furious will have grown too strong. This year is the Vikings' only chance.

A Hero must come to claim the Throne, with all of the Lost Things, by the eleventh day of Doomsday...

...Or all is lost.

# PROLOGUE BY HICCUP HORRENDOUS HADDOCK III, THE LAST OF THE GREAT VIKING HEROES

These last two books of my memoirs take place over ninety-six hours, during the last four days of Doomsday when I was fourteen years old, and I warn you that they are the darkest and most terrifying, and were the most difficult to write. For this was the time in which I faced both Grimbeard the Ghastly's Guardian Protectors of Tomorrow and the true might and anger of the dragon Furious.

This was the time in which the dragons faced extinction.

At the beginning of this book, war has come to the Archipelago, the dragons and the humans are trying to obliterate each other, and I am being hunted down by both the terrible dragons of the dragon rebellion, and the witch and Alvin the Treacherous.

I look back at that pale, skinny fourteen-year-old boy-who-once-was-me, and I feel such anxiety for him, for he does not yet know what is coming to him. He is living through this dreadful war, so he has seen death already, but he has not yet lost someone whom he loves. He is beginning to understand what it means to bear the burden of the guilt and responsibility of being a leader. But he has not yet accepted that burden as his fate and his destiny.

Will he be able to save the dragons in the end?

I yearn to help him.

I want to reach out across the chasm of space and stars and time and hold his hand to help him through it. But of course he is living in the past, that distant country, and however hard I shout, he will not hear me.

Now that I am an old, old man, looking back on my life, I can see the pattern and the reason for the darkness of that time.

Great things are only made out of love and out of pain.

A great sword must be made out of the very best steel. But what truly makes the sword great is what happens to the sword *after* it is made.

We call this the "testing" of the sword.

The sword is bashed and hammered and hollered into shape by the bright hammer. It is thrust into the fierce heat of the fire, where it softens, and then it is quickly quenched in water, where it hardens again. The higher the temperature, the fiercer the fire, the tougher and the greater the sword eventually becomes.

The whole testing process can make a sword, or break it.

The same could be said for the making of a Hero.

# 1. YOUR MOTHER SAID NOT TO LEAVE THE HIDEOUT

It was a chilly and foggy night in the Murderous Mountains.

A good night for treachery.

Humans should not have been out in the forests of the Murderous Mountains in those times of war. If the dragons of the dragon rebellion caught even one *hint* that there were humans moving in the burned trees of those misty mountain passes, they would hunt them down and kill them.

But somewhere deep in that forest, far away from any aid, a terrified human voice was shrieking, "*Help! Help! Help!*" and a little party of brave but foolish humans and dragons had set out to offer their assistance.

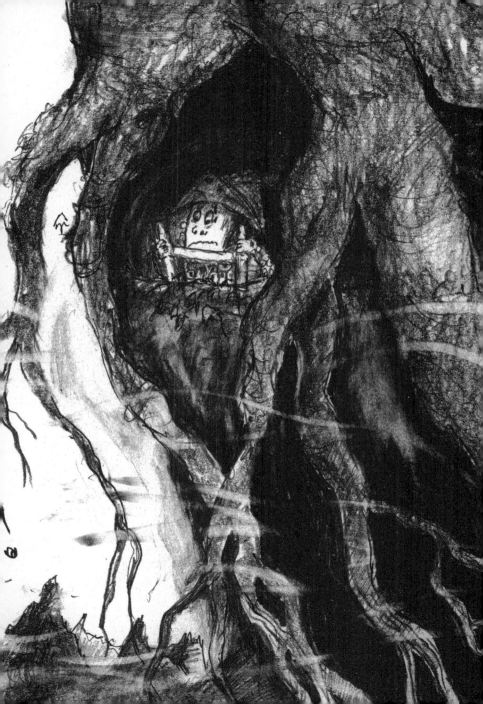

Hiccup Horrendous Haddock the Third was sitting on the back of a Deadly Shadow dragon, flying so low over the treetops that every now and then the slow downward beats of the dragon's wings brushed the scorched topmost twigs of the trees.

Deadly Shadow dragons are chameleons, and so this beautiful three-headed dragon was exactly the color of the midnight sky, complete with stars slowly shifting across its shining sides.

Hiccup's knees were trembling with the effort to keep a grip on the saddle.

Hiccup was a very ordinary-looking boy for one sought after by so many people. A ragged little string bean of a teenager, his Fire-Suit torn to ribbons, his face bruised and scratched, with the wild hair and scared eyes of one who had been

Hiccup
Haddock
III
↓

hunted by too many for too long. War and exile had turned him into a scarecrow of a boy.

His ears were ringing from the piercing coldness of the biting wind, and he was peering over the Deadly Shadow's necks as it flew, his heart beating horribly quick at the blackened wasteland down below. He was trying to work out where that piteously shrieking voice was coming from.

"*Help! Help! Help!*" screamed the voice, and now they could see the little flaring light of a campfire, burning deep in the woods, flickering on and off like a firefly, or the flickering of your curiosity.

Camicazi

Fishlegs

Windwalker

The Ten
Companions
of the
Dragonmark

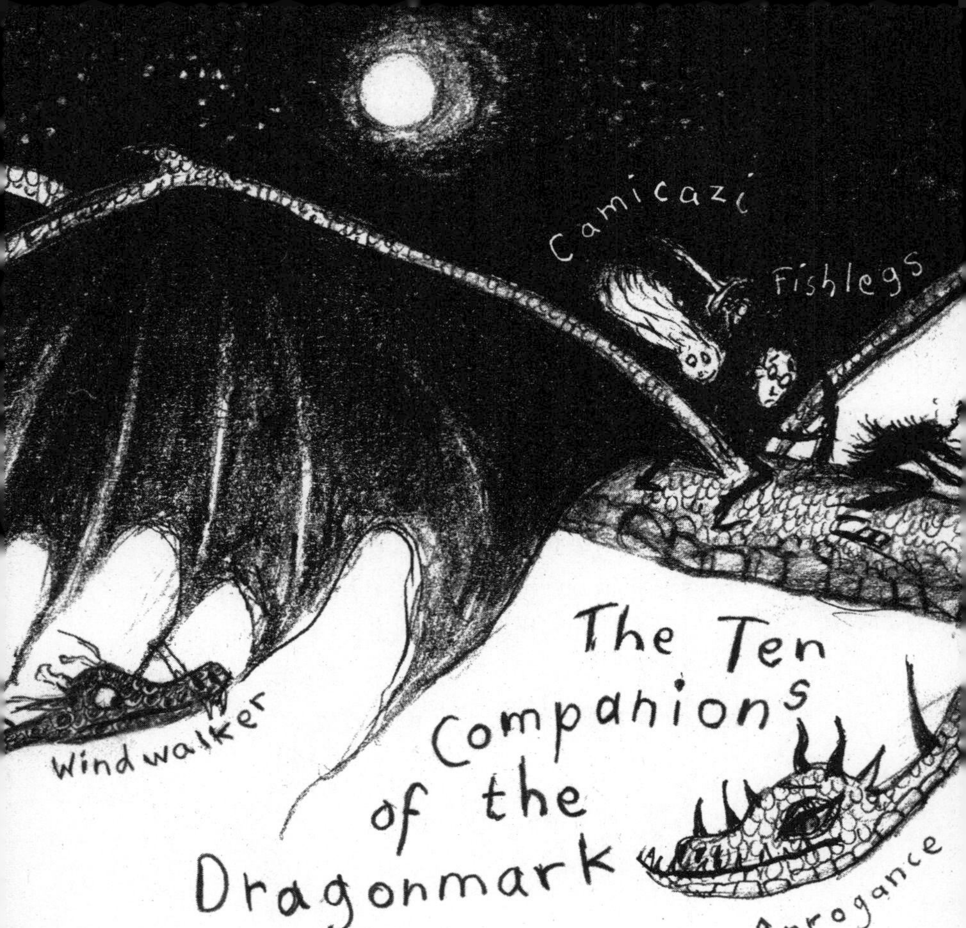

Arrogance

No wonder Hiccup was nervous, for this was the scorched, fire-ravaged territory of the dragon Furious and the dragon rebellion, and the dragon Furious was hunting more than anything for Hiccup, and Hiccup alone. The dragon Furious had made a solemn pledge to turn this world to ashes looking for him.

6

Hiccup

Innocence

Wodensfang

Patience

Toothless

He had sworn that no rock, no island, no cave nor cliff would be a safe hiding place for the boy. The results of the dragon Furious's crazed lunatic hunt lay in the melted, mutilated landscape around them, the ragged corpses of the trees, the burned remains of the smashed-up cliffs.

Stormfly

"Oh for Thor's sake," whispered Hiccup's best friend, Fishlegs, who was sitting behind him on the Deadly Shadow.

Fishlegs was, if anything, even skinnier and more ragged than Hiccup. His smashed glasses were perched perilously on the end of his nose. "We could be torn to pieces by the dragon rebellion! Your mother said ON NO ACCOUNT TO LEAVE THE HIDEOUT," protested Fishlegs. "We just need to stay in hiding for two more days, until Doomsday Eve, when we meet

the rest of the Dragonmarkers at the Singing Sands
of the Ferryman's Gift. That's ALL we need to do.
Your mother said she would take care of everything
else…"

"But what if it were one of us
all alone out there in that forest?"
Hiccup argued.

"You're right," said Fishlegs, getting a good trembling grip on his sword. "I know you're right…It's just that it's so scary…"

Hiccup and his two human friends were as white as grubs, having not seen daylight for a month. This was the first time they had been outside in all that time. Their dragons had taken turns to venture out and collect food and firewood. Now the Ten Companions of the Dragonmark had crept out of the safety of their hideout at the sound of that distant, terrified human voice.

As they swooped nearer to the little light, the desperate sound of the human voice came closer and closer, and it was impossible not to respond to the fear in that voice. What could be happening to that human to make him or her scream like that?

*"Help! Help! Help!"*

A human calling out to another human cannot be ignored.

Hiccup swallowed, looking at the trees below him. This once had been a living, breathing forest. Now it was as still as death, scorched and burned and wasted by the intensity of the dragon Furious's anger.

The third human on the Deadly Shadow's back was a small, fierce little Bog-Burglar called Camicazi. Her hair looked as if a family of over-excitable squirrels had been having an all-night party in the back of it.

"Oh come on, Fishlegs," whispered Camicazi, whistling happily. "You know we have to do this. Besides, *I* feel like a bit of exercise. We've been cooped up in that hideout for way too long."

Frankly, at this point, Camicazi had grown so fed up that if Hiccup had suggested hang gliding off the toe-talons of the dragon Furious she'd have been up for it.

*I feel like a bit of exercise.*

This is not some kind of Viking version of Girls keep Fit...

"A bit of exercise?" blustered Fishlegs. "A bit of exercise? This is not some kind of Viking version of Girls Keep Fit!"

Three little hunting dragons and one riding dragon were flying just above the Deadly Shadow. Two of the hunting dragons belonged to Hiccup: a very old one, the Wodensfang, with wings all tattered and torn; and a very young one, Toothless, the smallest, naughtiest hunting dragon in the Archipelago. The third hunting dragon was a golden chameleon Mood Dragon called Stormfly, and she belonged to Camicazi.

The riding dragon, the Windwalker, was a long-limbed, gentle, raggedy creature. He wagged his flag of a tail, hopefully waiting for everyone else to decide what to do.

"L-l-let's go home..." wept Toothless, in

Dragonese, the language that dragons speak to one another. Only Hiccup could understand him, for Hiccup was a dragon whisperer.

Toothless's huge green eyes were bulging wide in terror. He didn't really care about stranger-humans who didn't belong to him. He just wanted to go home, but he didn't want to admit it in front of Stormfly. Toothless was rather in love with Stormfly, so he tended to show off in her company.

"Is too ch-ch-chilly to b-b-be outside..." wept Toothless.

Toothless had a stammer, but this was even more pronounced because he was shivering so hard.

"Well, I told you to wear your coat, Toothless, didn't I?" Hiccup countered. "I told you and told you! But you said, oh no, you'd be too hot in your coat..."

L-l-let's go home...

Toothless (Hiccup's naughty hunting dragon)

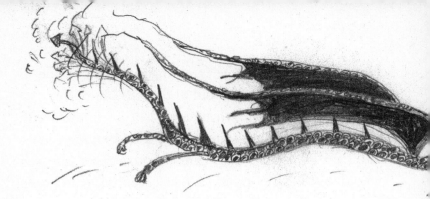

"That c-c-coat is *s-s-sissy*..." Toothless objected. "And actually T-t-toothless n-n-not cold after all...T-t-toothless very w-w-warm...but maybe a little t-t-too warm...Toothless needs to go back to the hideout so he can c-c-cool down..."

The too-warm Toothless was in fact so cold he had turned almost blue.

"Is not because T-t-toothless scared of the dragon rebellion dragons," huffed Toothless. "No, no, NO. Toothless can fight dragon rebellion dragons with one wing tied behind his back—yes, I can, Stormfly," he bragged. "Can't I, Wodensfang? And Toothless once b-b-bit the dragon Furious SO HARD on the bottom that he cried...But Toothless a little bit hot and he's got iffy wings...LOOK..."

Toothless held out his wing and made the end of it go all floppy.

"Flippy-floppy, flippy-floppy..." cooed Toothless, in

"I think you look cute in your coat, Toothless."

a tone of tender self-consolation.

"Yes, I've got a kind of tickly feeling in the back of my throat myself," hissed Stormfly, batting her naughty eyes. Stormfly spoke in Norse, for she was one of the very rare dragons who could speak the human tongue. "Maybe we should go back and have a little lie-down...Maybe I should go back and get Toothless's coat...I think you look quite cute in your coat, Toothless."

"Ooh, do you?" said Toothless, rethinking the coat.

"Nonsense, you'll feel all the better for some nice night air," scolded Camicazi. "It's probably indigestion in your case, Stormfly. You've got to stop swallowing those squirrels whole."

"INDIGESTION?" huffed Stormfly, outraged. Her beautiful serpentine body was currently purple (the color she turned when she lied), but as she grew angry, a haze of black mist fanned outward from her heart, like a cloud of ink slowly spreading through water. "INDIGESTION? I am an artist, a free spirit…I go where the wind takes me…Free spirits do not get *indigestion…*"

"I think I should warn you that this might be a trap, set for you by Alvin and his followers, the Alvinsmen," the Wodensfang warned Hiccup in a wheezy whisper.

The Wodensfang was a wrinkled brown leaf of a dragon who looked a little like a decrepit, droopy little dachshund that had shriveled like a raisin. His ears had gone purple and were shivering, which was what always happened when DANGER was near.

"Take the advice of my thousand years, Hiccup," said the Wodensfang. "That light is behaving very strangely if it is a campfire. I've never seen a campfire that moves…not in a thousand years, I haven't."

The Wodensfang was right.

The campfire was moving, slowly, slowly, down the length of the valley. Sometimes it was extinguished entirely by the heavy, shifting fog, or snuffed out by the denseness of the thickets of trees. But then it would flicker into life again, slowly and steadily, just a little bit farther down.

A campfire that moved?

Surely that was impossible!

The human voice had stopped shouting now. Somehow that was even more petrifying. Had its owner been snuffed out and swallowed by whatever terrors might lurk in this still, scarred landscape?

They were catching up with the light; it was bigger and brighter and stronger, and Hiccup could catch that distinctive smell of campfire in his nostrils.

They were now following the river that wound its way like a sinister sleeping snake through the center of the gorge.

The river turned a corner. And there it was...

A campfire, burning on an island of ice that was moving swiftly in the current in the middle of the river.

Lying on his front on the island of ice was a human, chained to a sleeping riding dragon, a Hurricane, with scars and whip marks all along its side.

Hiccup could see immediately why this human had been screaming. Running along the riverbanks, flitting through the trees, were the dark shapes of a

HELP! HELP

gigantic pack of Wolf-fangs. The human must have been camping on some frozen lake upriver, and the ice had broken up in the night and carried him on his little raft downstream, where his scent was picked up by Wolf-fangs. Wolf-fangs were neutral dragons, thank Thor, not part of the rebellion. They were flightless, but persistent killers nonetheless.

Some of them were already in the water, silently trying to climb on the raft, evil tongues hanging out, and the human was desperately knocking them back with his sword.

Well, that explained why the human *had been* screaming.

But why had he *stopped* screaming?

And why were those Wolf-fangs, scrabbling to get on board that ice raft, pursuing their prey without howling, without making a sound?

Oh for Thor's sake, oh for Thor's sake...

The human had stopped screaming because there was something else camped out overnight along the riverbanks, a lot of something elses that were still sleeping there, and these something elses were much worse than the Wolf-fangs.

With a sort of horror, Hiccup realized that what he *thought* had been fallen tree trunks lying just below the waterline in the rushes, in the shallows, weren't tree trunks at all.

They were Razorwings and Tongue-twisters, Brainpickers and Savagers, some of the scariest dragon species of the dragon rebellion.

And there weren't just a few of them, either.

*There were dragon rebellion dragons submerged all along the riverbanks as far as the eye could see.*

20

All around, in the shallows, were the still, sleeping, panther-like shapes of the dragons cooling their furnace-like bodies in the ice-cold currents of the river. A sickly, sulfurous yellow-green mist curled its way up from their bodies as the heat of their scales met the chill of the water.

One huge Savager was gnawing at the ragged remains of a gigantic tree in his sleep, a tree torn violently and entirely out of the ground, its poor tender roots spilled out like a desecration. Another, a Brainpicker, was holding the pathetic remnants of a bloodied human coat that Hiccup sincerely hoped did not belong to a Dragonmarker.

Their dark, sinister shapes oozed with menace and fear.

Hiccup urged the Deadly Shadow downward, trying to catch up with the poor, terrified human on the ice raft moving swiftly down the river below them.

Three pairs of human eyes and seven pairs of dragon eyes squinted through the mist to look at the human laid out full-length on his stomach on the moving island of ice, bashing away at the noses of Wolf-fangs trying to climb on board his raft and drag him under.

It was a man. A young man.

A young man who had lost hope that anyone

21

would rescue him now, and you could see from his defeated, terrified face that he thought he was about to die.

Hiccup caught his breath in shock as he recognized the human.

It was Snotlout.

"Help!"

# 2. "WE WERE JUST WONDERING WHOSE SIDE YOU ARE ON"

Hiccup was as shocked to see Snotlout there as if someone had hit him suddenly in the stomach. Snotlout was Hiccup's cousin, and he had been Hiccup's enemy ever since Hiccup was born.

When they last saw Snotlout on the battlefield back in the Amber Slavelands, Snotlout was trying to decide whether to be on their side or the side of Alvin and the witch. So which side had he chosen?

It appeared that Camicazi and Fishlegs thought they knew the answer to that question already.

"Let's get back to the hideout," whispered Camicazi in disgust.

Fishlegs sighed. "I'm afraid I agree."

"Hang on a second!" whispered Hiccup. "We can't just GO HOME and leave Snotlout here!"

Fishlegs looked at Hiccup with the hollow eyes of someone who has been on the run from the dragon rebellion for too long.

"Hiccup," said Fishlegs, "I don't think that Snotlout will have chosen to be on the Dragonmarker side. He is a lying, two-faced, treacherous villain who has betrayed you more times than I can remember, and he is almost certainly working for the Alvinsmen."

"People can change!" said Hiccup, his eyes lit up with enthusiasm. "You have to believe in people, and then maybe they can change!"

Fishlegs kept count on his fingers. "Let's see. He tried to kill you back in that swordfighting at sea lesson. He tried to kill you when we were on Hysteria that time. He threw the stone that revealed you had the Slavemark back in the School of Swordfighting... He just keeps betraying you again and again."

"This time it's going to be different," whispered Hiccup optimistically. "This time I'm *sure* he's changed...I'm convinced of it."

"If you try to save Snotlout," warned the Wodensfang, looking very nervous, "you will put us all in peril. By being kind to Snotlout, you may be endangering the lives of those who are loyal to you, who have never betrayed you. Sometimes kindness can be cruelty. These are the kinds of difficult decisions that a leader has to make."

Oh, thank you, Wodensfang. Very helpful. I may have mentioned this before, but: *Most of us are lucky not to be Kings and Heroes because we do not have to make the choices that Kings and Heroes have to make.*

# Razorwings

## ~ STATISTICS ~

**FEAR FACTOR:** ........................... 9
**ATTACK:** ................................. 8
**SPEED:** .................................. 8
**SIZE:** ................................... 7
**DISOBEDIENCE:** ...................... 7

These are very unpleasant dragons with wings so razor-sharp they can decapitate their victims in a heartbeat. Razorwings can turn themselves as flat as a spinning blade, and for good measure, they are also armed with darts that are mildly poisonous.

# Hogflys

## ~ STATISTICS ~

**FEAR FACTOR:** ........................... 0
**ATTACK:** ...................................... 1
**SPEED:** ......................................... 2
**SIZE:** ............................................. 2
**DISOBEDIENCE:** .................... 1

Hogflys are very gentle and eager to please;
however, they are one of the stupidest
dragon species in the entire dragon world.
They do have an extraordinary sense of
smell, so they can make very good tracker
or scent dragons, if you can overcome their
profound stupidity.

Sniff
Sniff

The ice raft creaked as one of the Wolf-fangs tipped it. Was it Hiccup's imagination, or did the dragons submerged along the edges of the riverbanks move too at the sound of that groaning ice?

At that moment, Hiccup noticed a very small, very ugly, miniature scent dragon sleeping innocently beside Snotlout and the Hurricane on the ice. It looked like a happy little pig. It was called a Hogfly, and Hogflys are the stupidest, most good-natured dragons in the entire world.

Nine pairs of eyes, dragon and human, looked at Hiccup anxiously. Hiccup loved his friends. It was his responsibility to keep them safe. But he couldn't leave a fellow human being, even if he was on the other side, let alone a poor, scarred riding dragon and a sweet, stupid little Hogfly, to a horrible fate at the talons of the dragons of the dragon rebellion.

"Let's save him," whispered Hiccup. "Let's save him!"

"Oh brother," moaned Fishlegs. "I know you're right, but oh brother…"

"We'll have to try to rescue him from above," said Hiccup. "I'll get the Deadly Shadow flying directly above the ice raft, and then Camicazi can let down a rope for Snotlout to climb up."

Let me just say that I COMPLETELY disagree with this decision!

"Let me just say that I completely disagree with this decision!" whispered Camicazi fiercely. "This is **MADNESS**! This is **CRAZY**! You've really lost the plot now, Hiccup, you Hooligan half-wit…" In one of her instant, bewildering turns of mood, she drew her sword. "I'd better go down there," she resolved.

I'd better go down there…

Before anyone could stop her, Camicazi tied a rope to the Deadly Shadow's saddle and, as soon as they were in place, lowered herself until she was hovering above the ice-island like a little black spider.

"Was that part of the plan?" Fishlegs asked.

"Suffering scallops, no! *Camicazi!*" Hiccup hissed. "Get back up here!"

But Bog-Burglars can be surprisingly deaf when they want to be.

"Ask him whose side he's on!" Fishlegs whispered helpfully from above.

Camicazi dangled from the rope below the Deadly Shadow dragon just above Snotlout's head. Holding on to the rope with one hand and stringing her bow with the other, she shot a Wolf-fang one-handed (one of Camicazi's more show-offy moves).

"Hello there," she said cheerily to Snotlout. "*Hiccup* thinks we should help you, but what *Fishlegs* wants to know is, whose side are you on? Because if you're on the side of the Alvinsmen, I will just leave you to it…"

Snotlout was busy fighting off the Wolf-fangs, but he whipped around his head in amazement as he heard this voice coming out of nowhere, and let out a small, surprised noise of astonishment.

Camicazi gave Snotlout a little, soothing wave and her biggest, brightest smile. Snotlout goggled at her, for she appeared to be dangling in midair, and for a second he thought he was seeing things. But then, pointing a shaking finger at the terrifying sight of the dragons sleeping in the riverbanks, he mouthed with dazed relief: "HELP ME...but be quiet..."

Camicazi ignored this, talking in her perfectly normal voice. "Yes, that's interesting you should ask for that, because we were just wondering whether to help you," explained Camicazi, swaying chattily above him.

"For Thor's sake,
you little Bog-Burglar
madwoman, those are
dragon rebellion dragons!
Have you seen what those
dragons have done to this
forest? And if they wake up, they
could call the dragon Furious!"

Camicazi dropped down
from the rope and landed like
a little cat on the ice-raft beside
Snotlout.

"You haven't answered
the question," said Camicazi.
"Whose side are you on?"

Snotlout made a frustrated, inarticulate gurgling noise as he bashed away at the paw of a grinning Wolf-fang who had nearly made it onto the raft.

"Okay," he rasped, "I'm on YOUR side! Most definitely on YOUR side! Indisputably on YOUR side! I came up here to find you so I could take you to the witch's camp so that you can find the rest of the Lost Things…"

"He says he's on OUR side!" Camicazi shouted up. "But I wouldn't trust him farther than I could throw him."

"I *told* you!" whispered Hiccup from above. "But keep it down a bit, Camicazi…"

"Are you quite sure that we should save him?" asked Camicazi wistfully. "He really is not very nice."

"Can't you speak *quietly*, you horrible little Bog-Burglar?" hissed Snotlout. "Uh-oh…"

"Uh-oh…" said Hiccup.

"Uh-oh?" groaned Fishlegs, who had covered his face with his hands in horror. "What do you mean, *uh-oh*? UH-OH is never good. Please take back that *uh-oh*, and give me, instead, a hearty, relieved *hoorah*. I hardly dare ask, but what's wrong?"

"The Hogfly," Hiccup explained. "I think the Hogfly is waking up…"

"Well, what's wrong with that?" Fishlegs whispered back. "Hogflys aren't dangerous."

The HOGFLY
Woke up with happy,
Splashing sneezes.

Too late.

The Hogfly woke up with three wet, splashing sneezes. It bounced up from the stomach of the sleeping Hurricane and shot out its wings so it hung in the air, buzzing like a fat pink bumblebee, its curly pink tail wagging vigorously as it looked to the left and right.

"WOOF! WOOF! WOOF!" barked the happy Hogfly.

The Hogfly was so stupid it thought it was a dog.

Was there a stiffening of the dragon rebellion

WOOF!
WOOF!

dragons all along the riverbanks at the sound of that last jolly little bark?

"Hogfly!" Hiccup whispered down to the Hogfly.

"Yoo-hoo!" the Hogfly called back, waving an exuberant pink trotter. "I can se-e-e-e-ee you! Hello, Grandma! Where's the toothbrush?"

It buzzed back and forth, its snout snuffling up and down.

And this time there was a *definite* quiver from the dragon rebellion dragons all along the riverbanks, limbs moving, eyes on the edge of opening.

"OOOOOH!" sang the Hogfly, its little snout trembling in excitement as it recognized Hiccup's scent. "I KNOW THAT SMELL! I WAS LOOKING FOR YOU! I WAS TRACKING YOU!" shouted the Hogfly, and to Hiccup's anxious ears, that shout was about as quiet and peaceful as the honking bellow of his old teacher, Gobber the Belch, umpiring a bashyball game, or the love-call of a giant Walrus-bog calling out to another lovesick Walrus-bog across a mile or two of ice floes.

"Me and the human-with-the-big-nose were playing a game and I was looking for you, tracking

YOO-HOO!

you all the way up the river! *Look,
human-with-the-big-nose!*" sang
the Hogfly triumphantly to Snotlout,
pointing at Hiccup with all four of its
trotters. "I'VE FOUND HIM! I'VE
FOUND HIM! I'D KNOW THAT
SMELL ANYWHERE!"

"Can't you shut that thing up?" hissed
Snotlout, bug-eyed with terror.

"Hogfly!" Hiccup whispered
down from the Deadly Shadow's back.
"Well done, clever you, but we're
playing a DIFFERENT game now...a
very DIFFERENT game...The new game
is the being-as-quiet-as-possible game...It's a
really fun one. Will you play with us?"

"Oooh, I'll play!" squeaked the Hogfly. "Let
ME play! Look at me playing!"

"Quiet as possible...quiet as possible..."
reminded Hiccup, putting a finger up to his mouth.
"Ssshhhh..."

The Hogfly concentrated very hard, clamped its
little mouth shut, and held its breath, turning purple
until it had swelled to almost three times its size, before
deflating suddenly with a loud POP! and opening its
eyes again in surprise.

"Pardon me...Is it your birthday? I WON!"
squealed the Hogfly.

"Yes yes yes yes yes..." whispered Hiccup,
looking nervously at the edge of the river. "But
*remember, quiet as possible...quiet as possible...*"

"Quiet as possible..." repeated the Hogfly
good-naturedly. "Tee-hee-hee...This is a very funny
game."

It concentrated very hard again, holding its
breath and hovering in the air, and swelling two, three
times. Hiccup bent down from the back of the Deadly
Shadow and tried to catch it, for it was floating within
arm's reach, but just as he made a grab for it...

POP!

The Hogfly deflated again, zooming out of the
reach of Hiccup's outstretched arm and tumbling
around in circles in the air, shrieking with giggles.

"PARDON ME! How's your father? *I* WON!
*I* WON! *I* WON!"

The revolting
dragon rebellion
dragons were moving
restlessly in their sleep.
The Hogfly
fluttered innocently up
to one grisly little group:

POP!

a Tongue-twister with its giant, hairy tongue hanging
out, a Brainpicker with its "pick" fixed into the head of
a poor dead badger, and a Razorwing sleeping low and
evil in the shallows like a lurking velociraptor, its
body submerged but its razor-sharp wings skimming
the shallows.

Happy and giggly and bustly, the Hogfly
ignored Hiccup's strangled cries
of: "*Hogfly! Come back here,
Hogfly!*"

"Ooh!" it
squeaked in
delighted confusion.
"*You all look so
lovely! How am I to
choose which one of you
to be my friend?*"

*Oooh,... you ALL look so lovely ...*

It perched on
the sinister swoop of the Razorwing's nose.

"*Where's my biscuit? Are you married? Be my
valentine...*"

"I can't bear to watch…" groaned Fishlegs.

It was like seeing an enthusiastic bunny
rabbit trying to make friends with a heavily armed,
bunny-eating cobra.

The Razorwing did not open its eyes.

But slowly, slowly, *slowly*, its jaws opened a tiny, *tiny* crack.

And out of the jagged crook of its mouth, like the noise from a ventriloquist's dummy, came a horrible, screechy little croaking voice, speaking very, very softly:

"MAKE RED your claws
with HUMAN BLOOD...
OBLITERATE the HUMAN FILTH..."

"Ooh, that's a nice song," said the Hogfly, ever polite, but suddenly a little nervous and confused, for the song of the Red-Rage is not a *nice* song at all.

"Torch the humans like a WOOD..."

And all around the riverbanks, the other dragon rebellion dragons did not open their eyes, but their mouths, with similar croaky voices, joined in this disgusting robotic chant.

"Oh brother…oh brother…" whispered Fishlegs.
"Here we go…this is going to be bad…"

The dragons began the chant again, louder
this time.

And…

SNAP!

One eyelid of the Razorwing snapped open, and
the eyeball of the Razorwing fixed on the Hogfly with a
thoughtful gaze just about as kindly and as reasonable
as the stare of a great white shark.

The Tongue-twister dragon opened its eyes simultaneously and stretched out its long, repulsively thick and hairy tongue toward the Hogfly's frantically blurring wings, hoping to twist one of them off. I am sorry, but it's true.

Slowly, slowly, the cavernous jaws of the Razorwing opened to their widest extent, to reveal two little poisoned darts lurking like little evil gnats in the fire-holes at the back of its throat.

This time, when the chant got to the part about "torching the humans like a wood," the poor, stupid little Hogfly *finally* realized what was happening. These dragons were not friendly or nice dragons at all. In fact, they were quite the opposite.

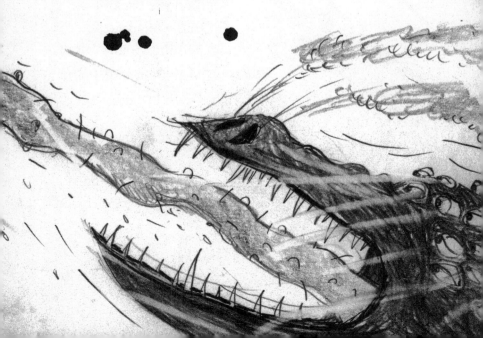

Its expression of good-natured bewilderment turned instantly to absurd alarm. Its jaunty little tail uncurled in drooping dismay as it backed away, whimpering, "Sorry, Uncle...Where's the exit? Did someone sneeze? Bite the bullet! *ABANDON SHIP!*"

Swooping down invisibly on the back of the Deadly Shadow, Hiccup snatched the Hogfly out of the air, put it in his backpack, and soared upward again immediately.

In the absolute nick of time, for:

ZING! ZING!

Little electric-yellow and ink-black darts whizzed over their heads as the Razorwing exhaled swiftly from his fire-holes.

The only good thing that happened *then* was
that the Wolf-fangs stopped attacking the ice-raft.
At the first sign that the rebellion had woken up, the
Wolf-fangs sprinted away and melted back into the
darkness of the mutilated forest, while the ones who
were in the river, with their snouts over the edge of the
raft, sank back down into the water and scattered like
fish. *They* knew trouble when they saw it.

Snotlout was not grateful to see the Wolf-fangs
disappearing. But then again, gratitude had never been
Snotlout's strong point.

"What are you doing, you jellyfish-brained
IDIOTS? Is this your idea of *rescuing* someone? You've
woken up the dragon rebellion dragons!" he hissed
in horrified disbelief. "And they're going to fetch the
dragon Furious!"

The situation spiraled out of control with
terrifying rapidity.

The dragons came out of their frozen, sleeping
stillness at the edges of the river into wild, frenzied life.
The hideous chant of the dragon rebellion exploded
around the young Vikings as the little ice-raft holding

Snotlout, Camicazi, and the sleeping Hurricane dragon sped downstream. The excruciating pitch and loudness of their battle hymn became in itself a form of attack. Screeching like harpies, the dragons screamed at decibel levels that were painful to the ears.

"*Rapids…*" breathed Hiccup in horror, looking down at the churning, foaming water and the sharp, evil-looking rocks ahead of Snotlout and Camicazi pointing upward like the devil's incisors.

And even worse, there was a distant booming, roaring sound, clearly audible in the still night air. What was that noise, that warning rumble like the beginning of a thunderstorm?

*Oh for Thor's sake.*

Hiccup suddenly remembered that when this particular river got to the ocean, it fell off the cliff in a gigantic waterfall that was the largest in the Archipelago.

"The waterfall!" yelled Hiccup, because there was no point trying to be quiet now.

"YOU HAVE TO GET OFF THAT ICE-RAFT BEFORE YOU HIT THE WATERFALL!"

# 3. PLAN GOING WRONG

The dragons of the dragon rebellion attacked with full mind-numbing force, their chant at an unbearable pitch, diving, swooping, shrieking, and shooting poisoned darts and terrible fire and shocking bolts of exploding lightning.

Camicazi and Snotlout fired arrows at the swooping horrors as they clung desperately to the tilting island of ice, bucking and speeding madly down the river like an out-of-control sleigh ride. Inexplicably, the Hurricane was still fast asleep.

The roar of the waterfall downstream got louder and louder, growing into a great watery din of noise, and even in the night air they could see a billowing mist of spray swelling up above the forest ahead, like clouds from a smoking volcano.

The waterfall was very close now. One more bend and they would be rocketing over the edge.

Hiccup and Fishlegs caused chaos and confusion by shooting at the attacking dragons from the back of the all-but-invisible Deadly Shadow. But the dragons were attacking in such nightmare numbers that it would be mere minutes before they overwhelmed the raft.

NE-OOOOW! Another Razorwing leaped from

the rocky riverbank and landed with an evil vulture grin
and a scrape of razored wings on the other end of the
ice-island, tipping it downward so violently that it was
practically submerged.

"This plan's going *really* wrong..." whispered
Camicazi as the Razorwing prepared to leap and slice
and—BAM!

The bucking, jostling island of ice slammed into
a rock and shattered into pieces...catapulting

Camicazi, Snotlout, the Razorwing, and the Hurricane
into the numbing cold of the river.

The freezing shock of the water woke the
Hurricane at last. With a screech of alarm, the poor
creature started swimming, trying to disentangle its wet
wings in the chaos of the raging rapids.

Snotlout was still attached to the Hurricane
by a long chain, and so he was dragged behind
the panicking riding dragon, buffeted over
and over and half drowned by the water.

Like an untidy scarecrow,
Fishlegs valiantly jumped
from the Deadly Shadow
and onto the Windwalker's
back so that he could help try
to catch Camicazi. Hiccup

urged the Deadly Shadow on, and Fishlegs flew the Windwalker down through the hail of Razorwing darts toward the blonde head of Camicazi bobbing in the river.

"DOWN, SHADOW! DOWN!" Hiccup shouted.

The triple-headed Deadly Shadow swooped... and missed, as a manic surge of water swept Camicazi out of the dragon's reaching talons.

ROOOOOOOARRR!

The sound of thousands and thousands of tons of gushing river water tumbling into a waterfall was absolutely terrifying, and it was just below them now.

The river rushed over the edge in a flooding, crashing tumult.

Just a second before she was swept over, Camicazi got one little monkey hand around the rope dangling from the Deadly Shadow above and was lifted clear of the deluge.

But the Hurricane went plunging over, plummeting

downward, and Snotlout and the Hurricane would have crashed to their deaths on the rocks below if the Hurricane had not dragged its wings out of the water in the nick of time. Screaming, the Hurricane soared upward, yanking Snotlout with him.

Fishlegs steered the Windwalker beneath the dangling Camicazi, and she dropped onto the Windwalker's back in midair. He then flew the Windwalker alongside the Hurricane, and Camicazi jumped onto the Hurricane's back so that she could heave the dangling Snotlout up on the chains and into the saddle.

The three dragons now wheeled about, and the Deadly Shadow shot back upriver toward the hideout in the mountains, closely followed by the Windwalker and the terrified snorting Hurricane and a pack of howling, murderous dragon rebellion dragons, driven mad by the arrow attack and sensing a meal on the horizon.

They didn't have long to get back to safety.

And now Hiccup heard a sound that *really* chilled his blood.

This was far worse than a mere waterfall. It was a distant, screaming, baying bawl, the inevitable result of the awful chant of the Red-Rage.

It was the roar of the dragon Furious.

One of the dragon rebellion dragons must have flown up to his stronghold in the north and awoken him. Even at this distance Hiccup could just make out the words:

"HE MUST NEVER GROW UP! I WILL HUNT HIM DOWN! I WILL SWOOP FROM THE HEAVENS AND OBLITERATE HIM!"

By "him" the dragon Furious was referring to Hiccup.

Far away to the north, out of that ice and that fire, those volcanic bubbling pools, there rose a dark shape so unimaginably large that it blotted out the moon. Each beat of his immense dark wings took it across a vast extent of territory at astonishing speed as it headed south, straight toward them in the Murderous Mountains, his eyeballs leaking fire, and his great mouth screaming murder and butchery and everything awful.

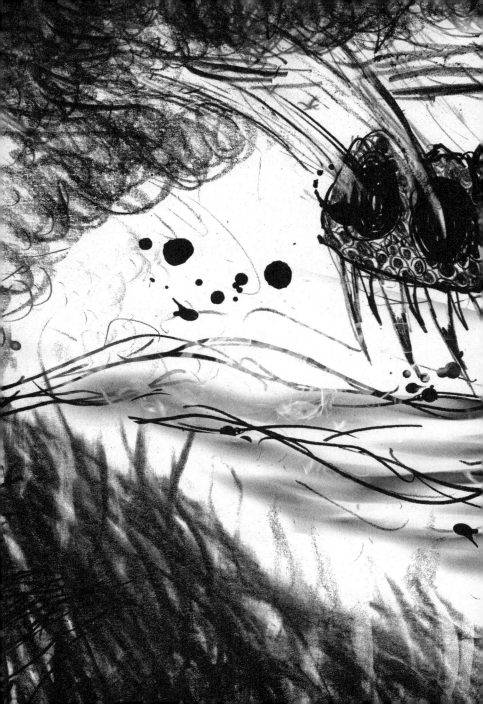

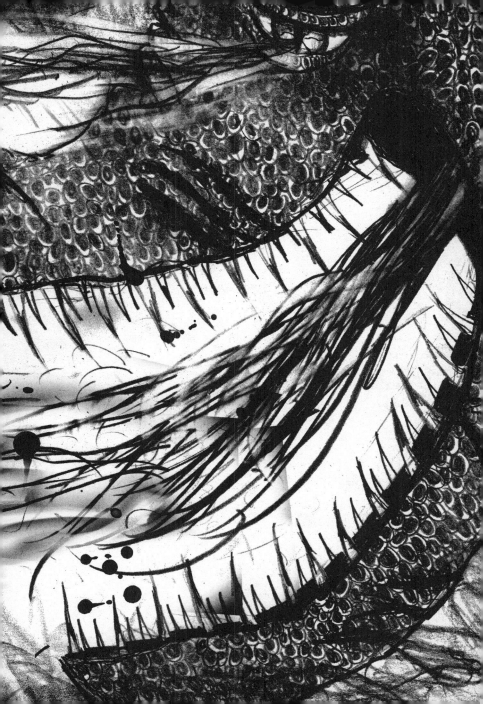

"We need to make it back to the hideout—*now!*"
Hiccup yelled hysterically.

There were so many dragons of the dragon
rebellion that they looked like a mass of
thunderclouds or a plague of locusts, thousands
and thousands and thousands strong.

They were flying so close to one another
that every now and then the Razorwings
accidentally sliced the head off any dragons
flying next to them, and scaly heads
dropped randomly into the gorge,
still screaming and shooting fire or
lightning or poisoned arrows.

Hiccup let the Deadly Shadow steer while he lay backward on his tummy like a rear gunner, firing arrows continuously at the pursuing dragon rebellion, trying to make sure he didn't accidentally hit Fishlegs on the Windwalker, or Snotlout and Camicazi on the Hurricane.

The flying conditions were extraordinarily difficult: the shifting fog; the zig-zagging, twisting gorge; and spindly, needlelike rock formations looming up unexpectedly out of the mist. It was a little like shooting rapids in the air.

Luckily, the Windwalker, the Deadly Shadow, and the Hurricane were some of the fastest riding dragons in the Barbaric World—only a Silver Phantom flies faster—so they just about kept ahead of the screaming, spitting, howling horror of the dragon rebellion in pursuit. Hiccup tried not to listen to the deeper, darker threat in the background, the great winged shape of the dragon Furious, whose ferocious bellow was even louder than the Red-Rage. Furious sailed nearer and nearer, like a great hunting owl of the nighttime, swooping down on some little mice that have incautiously left their mousehole for a second.

"I WILL TEAR THE WORLD APART IN THE HUNT FOR HIM! I WILL KILL HIM MYSELF!"

The Windwalker and the Deadly Shadow rounded a corner, and with passionate relief, Hiccup saw a gigantic spur of rock looming out of the fog right in front of them.

High up on a pointed pinnacle, with a breathtaking view over the entire surrounding landscape, there was a tree balanced so precariously on a clifftop that it was almost in the act of falling off. And beneath the tangled roots of this tree, there was the underground tree house camp so secret and so well hidden there were barely half a dozen beings alive in the world who were aware of its existence.

Alvin the Treacherous would have given his very best hook to know where that underground tree house was. The dragon Furious too had his dragons hunting high and low for it, day and night.

It had once been the underground hideout that Fishlegs's mother, Termagant, had made long ago when she was a little girl growing up in the Murderous Mountains. The Deadly Shadow, who had previously been Termagant's dragon, had shown it to them, and Hiccup and his friends had been

hiding there, waiting to meet up with the
Dragonmarkers on Doomsday Eve.

Hiccup had never been so glad to
see the hideout.

He hauled on the reins and
brought the Deadly Shadow to a
sudden, plunging halt in the air.

"Take the others to the
underground tree house and I'll
hold up the dragon rebellion!"
Hiccup shouted to Fishlegs as he
rocketed past on the back of the Windwalker. Thor
knows how much Fishlegs heard at the speed he was
going.

The Hurricane zoomed after Fishlegs on the
Windwalker in a maddened stream of terror. Hiccup
braced himself. He had six arrows lined up on the
Deadly Shadow's back, and he fixed one to his bow
with trembling fingers. Hiccup had the advantage of
the Deadly Shadow's invisibility, so that the dragon
rebellion dragons would not know where his arrows
were coming from.

Timing was everything.

The first dragon rebellion dragons plunged

The entrance to the
secret tree hideout
IS HERE.

around the corner, and Hiccup let fly one, two, three, four, five, six arrows.

With a shriek of shock, the first dragon, a Razorwing, was hit. It went spiraling into the pack behind and then plummeted down into the gorge. There was a brief, squalling moment of confusion. But it was enough. By the time the pack had righted themselves and recovered their concentration, their prey had disappeared.

The Windwalker, the Hurricane, and their riders had vanished down the entrance to the underground tree house, and the dragon rebellion, drooling and enraged, could not see Hiccup hovering only twenty feet away from them on the back of the Deadly Shadow, which had reared up to conceal its rider. The Razorwings swam in the air, barking at one another, and eventually set off farther down the gorge, where they supposed the prey must have gone.

Hiccup breathed again.

And then it happened.

# 4. TWO RED EYES, SUSPENDED IN THE AIR

There were two red eyes, suspended in the air, right in front of where the Deadly Shadow was hovering.

Red eyes, narrowed to slits, with the pupils slightly shivering.

Hiccup blinked, his brain unable to comprehend the sight of two red eyes floating before him.

In the heat of the dragon rebellion chase, he had forgotten that the humans—Alvin the Treacherous and his mother, Excellinor the witch—were also looking for Hiccup, and the witch was using Vampire Spydragons to hunt and spy for her.

Hiccup had never seen a Vampire Spydragon before, but he knew they were chameleons that could turn every part of themselves invisible—apart from their glowing red eyes.

Slowly the rest of the Vampire Spydragon materialized around those two red eyes hovering in front of Hiccup.

It was a ghastly shrieking creature, with the head of a vampire bat and the body of an enormous monkey.

For one second Hiccup saw this vision, and then there was a searing pain in his left arm. He looked down in confusion, as if it were happening to someone else, to see the head of the Vampire Spydragon attached to his arm.

The creature did not have time to latch on properly with its clamping jaws before the Deadly Shadow turned its head and tore the Vampire Spydragon off Hiccup, throwing the bloodsucker into the air like a dog tearing a rat off its back.

One second the screaming monster was visible—
the next it faded into invisibility again, red eyes
descending into the gorge.

Before Hiccup could move, or think, the flames
of the dragon Furious reached the forest.

"I WILL HUNT HIM DOOOOOOOWNNN!"

A great horizontal wall of fire blasted across
the night sky with such white-hot heat that it sheared
off the top of the mountain behind the underground
tree house. The entire summit, tons and tons of rock
and boulders, plummeted into the gorge below.

The three mouths of the Deadly Shadow

screamed simultaneously as the fire poured on and on
over their heads, and in a few swift flaps it shot through
the ivy-draped entrance to the underground tree house.

Just in time.

"He's been hit...He's been hit..." Hiccup
heard a shaking Fishlegs say as he helped Hiccup
down from the Deadly Shadow's back, and
because Hiccup was nearly fainting it
sounded like Fishlegs was talking from
a long distance away.

Outside,
the dragon Furious,
full of vengeful hope,
finally reached the place where
the boy had last been seen. But his
prey had disappeared, and Furious had
been robbed of his victory once again.

The dragon Furious exploded in an
armageddon of anger, and as the dragon
rebellion's fires of rage torched the battered
remains of the landscape below, a trembling
Toothless, Stormfly, and the Hogfly flattened
themselves against the walls of the hideout around
the entrance. The Wodensfang popped his little
ancient head above the hole to peer out and swiftly
ducked down again.

"He won't find us in here," wheezed the
Wodensfang, trying to reassure *himself* as much as
anyone else. "He won't find us...He's hunted
us before and he won't find us now..."

But it was difficult to stay calm as the Red-Rage rebellion struck, relentlessly terrible and unremitting. They could hear the burning and the crackling and the shrieking as the forest went up in flames again, and the wood shriveled up like paper, and the little forest creatures screamed as they fled the inferno.

"Camicazi…" panted Hiccup. "Where is Camicazi?"

"Hang on, Hiccup, you're wounded…" Fishlegs was winding something around Hiccup's arm. "Hang on…"

But Hiccup ignored him and staggered into the underground tree house's second room. Camicazi was not there.

Hiccup limped back through the rooms again and tried to climb the ladder up to the hole of the entrance, only to be blown back, almost like he had been punched in the face by a fist of heat. The wall of flame was so burning hot that it seared the skin, even a few feet into the room.

The Wodensfang shook his head gently.

"You can't go out there, Hiccup, not at the moment…"

"But we have to go after her!" panted Hiccup.

"Not now, Hiccup…"

"Where has she gone?" asked Fishlegs with round, solemn, horrified eyes.

"She was taken," said a voice from behind them.

There on the floor, still attached to the Hurricane by a long chain, lay Snotlout, his face hidden in shadow. He repeated the same words, in the same dead, flat voice. "She was taken."

"What do you mean, 'taken'?" asked Fishlegs.

Hiccup already knew what Snotlout was going to say.

A horrible lightning image of the Vampire Spydragon with the red eyes flashed into Hiccup's mind. It seemed to be laughing at him.

*If there was one Vampire Spydragon in that gorge, maybe there were more...*

"She was taken alive," said Snotlout, "by one of the witch's Spydragons."

# 5. THE BITE OF A VAMPIRE SPYDRAGON

"I saw it," said Snotlout quietly. "She showed me in here, but just before she climbed in after me, a Vampire Spydragon swooped down out of nothing and nowhere and it took her."

"Windwalker! Is this true?" Hiccup turned to the Windwalker, who was lying on the floor, his long, shaggy body riddled with Razorwing stings. Hiccup had some vague, desperate hope that the Windwalker might deny it, but the Windwalker gave a miserable nod and continued that low, keening whining.

"No…" whispered Hiccup. "Oh no…"

He put his arms around his thin white trembling body, trying to comfort himself. His arm sang with pain.

ALL MY FAULT.

Camicazi had trusted Hiccup's instinct over her own. She hadn't agreed with his decision, but trustingly, loyally, she had followed Hiccup into battle, and now she had been lost.

*She was taken.*

MY FAULT.

What had the Wodensfang said?

"If you try to save Snotlout," he had warned, "you will put us all in peril. By being kind to Snotlout, you may be endangering the lives of those who are loyal to you, who have never betrayed you. Sometimes kindness can be cruelty. These are the kinds of difficult decisions that a leader has to make."

"Well, what do you expect?" said the cold, hard voice of Snotlout contemptuously. "You made a complete bird's nest of the entire operation. You woke up the dragons of the dragon rebellion. The noise probably told the witch's Vampire Spydragons that we were there. What did you think was going to happen?"

Fishlegs was trembling with heaving anger, and he turned on Snotlout.

"We were only out there in the first place to save your poxy little life! Why didn't you at least try to go after her, Snotlout? She risked her life for you, and you couldn't even be bothered to follow her?"

"Of course, I was dying to go after the dear little Bog-Burglar brat," drawled Snotlout, "and I'd have jumped on my trusty steed like a shot. You know what a gentleman I am, Fishlegs, but my own riding dragon has most unfortunately been hit by Razorwing stings and can hardly move his wings."

"How do we know that YOU didn't hand over Camicazi to the witch? Maybe this has all been a trick to betray us to the Alvinsmen!"

Fishlegs's hot, angry words said aloud what Hiccup was thinking.

"Why did we listen to your cries for help? You probably gave her to the witch's Spydragon! And *you*," shouted Fishlegs, "are not worth even a tenth of that girl!"

Snotlout said nothing. His face was in darkness, but perhaps there was a quivering in his fingers when Fishlegs said he was not worth a tenth of Camicazi.

But then again, perhaps not.

"That little Bog-Burglar?" he drawled.

MY FAULT.

"Come on, she's only a Bog-Burglar, after all…"

It was as if Snotlout was deliberately trying to provoke them.

That was when Fishlegs really lost his temper.

Snotlout had bullied Fishlegs all his life. Anybody who has been bullied knows what that is like. Fishlegs had spent all of his first ten years in pure fear, too terrified to go out the door of his lonely little hut, in case he got caught by Snotlout and his bullying sidekick, Dogsbreath the Duhbrain, who would hit him, and kick him, and take no notice if he pleaded or cried.

And now they had saved Snotlout's life, and Snotlout had repaid them by betraying Camicazi, who was one of the only two human friends Fishlegs had ever had.

Fifteen years of being bullied, of hatred, of anger, welled up in Fishlegs.

All of Fishlegs's anxiety about where Camicazi might be, the fear of what the dragon Furious would do if he found them in that hideout, all of his rage at Snotlout came together in a white-hot rush.

"We should throw you out of the hideout!" roared Fishlegs. "You are a LIAR! You are a TRAITOR! You have betrayed Hiccup and us all, time and time again!"

The three heads of the Deadly Shadow let out a simultaneous scream, and lightning ricocheted around the inside of the cavern, and the three heads inhaled, ready to strike, for Fishlegs was their master now.

BAM! Fishlegs hit Snotlout, plumb on the nose.

Snotlout looked completely and totally astonished. He had never really thought much about that weed, Fishlegs, apart from thinking up clever ways to humiliate him. Fishlegs had never dared so much as to *pinch* Snotlout, let alone punch him. Snotlout raised his arms to hit back, and then paused as the gigantic Deadly Shadow's three heads screamed a warning.

BAM! Fishlegs hit him again.

Snotlout half laughed, because however hard Fishlegs tried to hit, his scrawny, weedy little arms were not really going to do any damage. That enormous three-headed monster of his, though…Well, *that* could do Snotlout some real damage. Snotlout eyed it fearfully.

"How does it feel," said Fishlegs through gritted, furious teeth, "to know you are completely at someone else's mercy?"

Not good, as it happened.

Snotlout looked at Fishlegs's howling, Berserk-like face, and at the dreadful, roaring three-headed nightmare of a Deadly Shadow beside him. He paled a little. "Come on now, Fishlegs," he said uneasily. "You can take a joke now, can't you? I was always only joking…"

"Oh, it was a joke, was it?" spat Fishlegs. "Well, then *I'm* just joking too! How does it feel to know that whatever you do, whatever you say, however you plead, someone is NEVER…GOING…TO…STOP?"
BAM! BAM! BAM!

Fishlegs hit him again and again and again.

"Stop!" said Hiccup, grabbing Fishlegs's arms. "STOP!"

Fishlegs finally stopped. The red rash of anger disappeared from his face and he dropped his arms.

*There is something truly dreadful about this war*, thought Hiccup, in weary horror. It had made even gentle, unwarlike Fishlegs, who wanted to be a bard, actually *strike* Snotlout in anger.

"Snotlout would kill us, wouldn't he? He has tried to kill *you*, on many occasions," said

Fishlegs flatly.
"You can't be
weak, Hiccup.
You can't give
him so many
second chances."

"That is the
way that Alvin and the
witch talk," said Hiccup,
flushed because he felt so
guilty about Camicazi, and
yet had a horrible suspicion
that Fishlegs might be right.
"You have to give people a
chance." He was still holding on to Fishlegs's arms.
"You have to *keep on* giving people a chance."

Fishlegs looked at Hiccup, startled.

And then Fishlegs sighed and pushed his
curly hair out of his eyes. The last peppery speck of
Berserk-anger faded from his cheeks, and he scratched
a little eczema patch inside his left elbow, and
whispered despairingly, "You're right…It's this war. It
does things to you after a while."

Snotlout was absolutely white, stiff with anger
and humiliation because he had been hit by that weed

*I don't know what came over me… It's this war.*

Fishlegs, and the three-headed Deadly Shadow dragon had actually scared him, and everyone in that cave had seen that he was scared.

"Talk about giving a Viking a bad name!" he jeered bitterly. "Talk about giving people a chance! I know we've been enemies in the past, but I too have risked my life to come up here to warn you, even to *help you*..." He shrugged his shoulders. "But if you don't want to believe me, then don't. See if I care!"

"Let's calm down," said Hiccup quietly. "We're not going anywhere at the moment. We can't find Camicazi until the dragon Furious goes away..."

*If the dragon Furious ever DOES go away, for it is sounding like he will not rest this time until he has fried us in our beds...*

"...and lots of us are wounded," said Hiccup. "Let's see to that, and then Snotlout can tell us his side of the story."

Most of the injuries were Razorwing poison darts, which had to be removed, leaving a numbing pain that hurt more than the sting of a bee or a hornet.

But more seriously, a great purple-black bruise, like a spreading flower, was making its way up Hiccup's left arm where the Vampire Spydragon had bitten him. And when Hiccup took away the rags that Fishlegs had wrapped around the wound a couple of minutes ago so that he could put some herbs on the injury to heal it, he started in horror.

The bite was not deep.

But a single tooth from the Vampire Spydragon was embedded inside his arm.

Hiccup was a dragon watcher, so he knew a great deal about the various dragon species, and the way they hunt.

Vampire
Spydragon
tooth embedded
in the arm acts as
a tracking device →

Vampire Spydragons catch their prey a little like Komodo dragons. They bite their victim, leaving one of their teeth in the wound, and let go. The poison in the bite then slowly paralyzes the prey, and the Vampire Spydragon locates its dying and helpless victim by the tracking device of its own tooth.

"Don't try to get the tooth out!" warned the Wodensfang. "Your body will work to reject it, and in time it will fall out naturally. The tooth has serrated edges, so if you try to dig it out in the meantime, you will just do yourself more damage.

"There will be a lot of numbness, paralysis even, for a bit, but it is not a deep bite, so you will not die. The same applies to the Razorwing stings—the stings are painful but not fatal..."

*But in the meantime, that Vampire Spydragon will be tracking me*, thought Hiccup.

Toothless had no real idea what was going on, but he understood that his master was upset, and lovingly he went and sat on Hiccup's head. "D-d-don't be sad, Master. Toothless is here," Toothless reminded him, sliding down to Hiccup's shoulders and putting his wings around Hiccup's neck with a tenderness that nearly strangled him.

Toothless searched for something that might cheer Hiccup up.

"I'll wear my c-c-coat if you like?" said
Toothless. "Look! Toothless will wear his coat...*That
will make you feel better...*"

He fetched his coat, which was half charred
because Toothless had hidden it helpfully in the fire.

"Does that make you feel better, Master?
Toothless is c-c-cute and he won't catch a cold now...
A-a-a-tishyoo!"

Toothless sneezed a large amount of dragon snot
right in Hiccup's face.

"W-w-whoops! Sorry..."

"Thank you, Toothless," lied Hiccup
automatically, wiping his face and putting a hand out to
the little dragon. "That makes me feel much better."

The Hogfly nestled under one
of Hiccup's arms and squeaked
sympathetically: "Tickle my
birthdays...It's bathtime...Hold
the peanut..." It didn't make
much sense, but Hiccup was
touched that both dragons,
in their different ways, were
trying to comfort him.

Snotlout watched
them all moving about,
quiet and sad, wounded

# Vampire Spydragons

## ~ STATISTICS ~

FEAR FACTOR: .......................... 8
ATTACK: ................................ 9
SPEED: .................................. 7
SIZE: .................................... 5
DISOBEDIENCE: ...................... 7

Vampire Spydragons are chameleons who can turn invisible apart from their red eyes. They have bodies of monkeys and heads of gigantic vampire bats. There is nothing more terrifying than being surrounded by floating red eyes in the darkness of a forest, which are often the last thing their victims see before they die.

and frightened, as the rage of the dragon rebellion roared on outside. At least they had one another. *He* was out of place and out of time, shut out from their companionship; an interloper, watching them from the shadows.

Snotlout had a deep cut on his right arm and one or two on his face, both near misses with a Razorwing's wings, but nobody was going to help him clean or dress his wounds. The hatred in the room toward Snotlout was so thick and heavy that you could reach out and touch it. Both dragons and humans avoided looking at him, as if he had a nasty smell. Snotlout had to tear bits off his own shirt and wind them around his gashes, and his pride made him pretend they didn't hurt too much.

*It is only that wimp Hiccup who is giving me a chance*, thought Snotlout resentfully.

"Does anybody feel like helping me *finally* pick the lock on my chain?" he drawled. "And then I can tell you my side of the story, and you may just find that I was on your side all along…"

"If you are on *our* side, where is your Dragonmark?" demanded Fishlegs, still very hostile. "Show it to us, you traitor!"

Snotlout coolly took off his helmet, to show a forehead entirely free of any tattoos whatsoever. "I have no Slavemark," said Snotlout. "But I am still on your side."

"HA!" snorted Fishlegs, and the dragons joined in the disbelief with smoky sniggers of derision.

"GIVE HIM A CHANCE TO EXPLAIN!" shouted Hiccup.

"Thank you," said Snotlout, bowing to Hiccup ironically.

# Conversations with Toothless

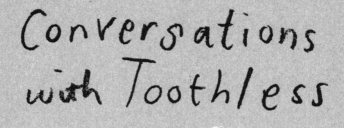

Your dragon can feel a little threatened when a new dragon enters the household. Be patient and he will get over it. Hopefully...

Toothless: Hogfly ne-ah com sweetie-giggly com T-T-Toothless.
*The Hogfly is not as cute as Toothless.*

You: Simple ne-ah, Toothless. TOOTHLESS si la mos xcellent oos. May noos ava be keendice a di fella.
*Of course not, Toothless. TOOTHLESS is the best one. But we have to be nice to him.*

Toothless: Simply, simply. Toothless willa be B-B-BIG-TIME keendice a di stupidissimo lacksmart greenblood.
*Of course, of course. Toothless will be VERY nice to him.*

Pause.

Toothless to the Hogfly: H-H-Hogfly, pishyou, yow goggle com un squealmunch plus yow est plusdim com un snot-trailer.

*Hogfly, please, you look like a pig, and you are more stupid than a snail.*

You: TOOTHLESS! *TOOTHLESS!*

Toothless (whining): May Toothless speekee pishyou! *But Toothless said please!*

Another pause.

Toothless: Hogfly, yow wantee a play hidey-plus-looky? Y-y-yow hide oppsthere wi di keendlee ickle Wettingsgreenblood undi Noddle-Scratchers, plus me adda a ponder o marvels und cum opps und loc yow...

*Hogfly, do you want to play hide-and-seek? You hide out there and play with the sweet little Sea-Dragon and the Brainpickers, and I'll count to a hundred million and then I'll come out and find you...*

Hogfly (tail wagging happily): Woof! Woof!

H-H-Hogfly
NoT as
Cute
as
Toothless

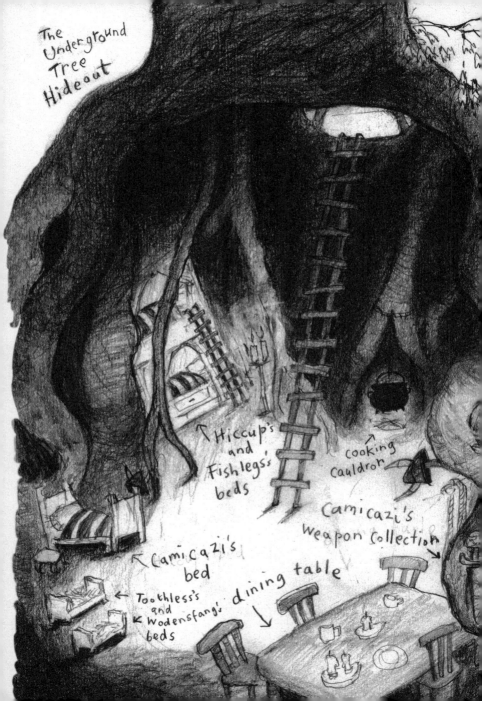

The
Underground
Tree
Hideout

Hiccup's and Fishlegs's beds

cooking cauldron

Camicazi's weapon collection

Camicazi's bed

Toothless's and Wodensfang's beds

dining table

# 6. THE OTHER SIDE OF THE STORY

"The Doomsday of Yule is in three days' time," said Snotlout. "And you are running out of time. I am presuming you have an agreement with Valhallarama that she will steal the nine Lost Things from Alvin, and then she will meet you on the Singing Sands of the Ferryman's Gift on Doomsday Eve and hand them over?"

"That's a very clever guess of yours, Snotlout," said Hiccup quietly. "My mother said all we had to do was stay in hiding and meet her there on Doomsday Eve."

"Well," said Snotlout, "Alvin's underground war bunker is hidden somewhere so clever, so secret, that Valhallarama and Stoick will never find it even if they search for a hundred years. So your mother, Valhallarama, and the Dragonmarkers have failed in their Quest to steal the other nine Lost Things from Alvin."

There was a short, depressed silence.

"Why should we believe you, Snotlout?" asked Fishlegs. "You could be lying. Valhallarama could already have the other nine things, and you could be sent here by the witch. If you joined our side, why didn't you get the Dragonmark?"

"Hiccup isn't the only one who uses his head, you know, Fish-eggs," replied Snotlout. "I thought I might be more use to the Company of the Dragonmark if I appeared to be working for the other side."

Stormfly gave a quick, soft hiss of reluctant approval. "Ah," she said. "Cunning and trickery. Good thinking." And then, remembering it was Snotlout speaking, she frowned again. "If it's true, of course."

"So I pretended to be on the witch and Alvin's side," said Snotlout.

"I let them take me to their hideout. I found out where they were keeping the things, and ran away to find you guys. I used this ridiculous Hogfly dragon here to help me track you down. Hogflys may be unbelievably stupid, but they are the best scent dragons in the world. I camped on a frozen lake upriver; the lake must have unfrozen in the night; the Wolf-fangs chased me...and that's when you found me."

"If you know where the Lost Things are," asked Fishlegs suspiciously, "why didn't you steal them *yourself*, when you escaped from Alvin's war bunker?"

"I couldn't do it on my own," explained Snotlout. "The things are guarded, and the Throne is heavy.

You lot are useless, of course, but I have to admit, your camouflaged-so-it-is-invisible and humongously enormous three-headed Deadly Shadow will come in useful in a burglary situation.

"Together we can steal back the things," continued Snotlout, "and even rescue that horrible little Bog-Burglar Camicazi. We can be at the beach at Hero's Gap on Doomsday Eve, with *all* the things, and then the Guardian Protectors of Tomorrow will make Hiccup the next King of the Wilderwest, and humanity will be saved."

"How do we know we can trust you?" asked Hiccup. "How do we know you're not going to betray us and deliver us straight into Alvin and the witch's hands?"

"I suppose," said Snotlout, "you don't. You'll just have to take my word for it. It's up to you. I don't really care *what* you believe anymore. If you want to think the worst of me, go ahead! I'm going to sleep now, if you don't mind. It's been a long couple of days."

Snotlout's clothes had dried entirely now, in the steamy warmth of that dragon-and-fire-warmed hideout. He yawned, wrapped himself up in one of Fishlegs's mother's old blankets, closed his eyes, and pretended to go to sleep.

But inside the blanket, his eyes were wide open.

"C-c-can Toothless bite him?" asked Toothless hopefully. "Or would that be rude? Does it matter being rude to a rude person? Or does it n-n-not count?"

"Yes, that would be rude, Toothless, so you can't bite him, although I'm feeling a bit tempted myself, I have to confess," admitted Hiccup.

"Suffering scallops," said Fishlegs in disgust. "What do we do now? Do we trust Snotlout or not? I still don't see why, if he's on our side, he doesn't have the Dragonmark."

"The Dragonmark is a symbol of SLAVERY!" said the muffled voice of Snotlout. "I'm on your side, but I don't want to be marked with a symbol of slavery!"

They all lay down to try to sleep, but this was difficult when they were all so angry, confused, and frightened.

"Did I make a mistake in rescuing Snotlout?" Hiccup asked the Wodensfang. "Is that why Camicazi was captured?"

The Wodensfang answered that question with another question.

"Can it *ever* be a mistake," replied the

Wodensfang, "for a human to answer the cry for help of another human?"

"Even if Snotlout is lying," said Hiccup in Norse, "he's the only one who knows where the witch's camp is. So we have to trust him anyway, because he's the only one who can lead us to Camicazi. Oh, I do hope she is all right."

"Yes, I know," said Fishlegs miserably. "I'm really worried about her too. I keep trying to tell myself that she's going to be all right...Look how many times she has escaped from prisons. She is an Escape Artist, after all..."

"Yes, but the witch and Alvin are getting worse," said Hiccup anxiously. "They've been killing people. I've seen Dragonmarker helmets hung from the trees of the forest outside as a warning that they are trying to claim this territory for the Alvinsmen..."

It was true.

Out in the forest there were long stakes, driven into the ground, and hanging on the end of each stake were either the heads of dragon rebels or Dragonmarker helmets that had been taken as trophies and put there to warn other Dragonmarkers that this land was claimed by Alvinsmen.

Quite apart from all these worries, the sounds of

the dragon Furious and the rebellion outside weren't
exactly a lullaby: that noise of the blackened remains
of the forest being torched once again, the flickering of
flames, the roar as they turned from flickers into a great
storming, roaring conflagration, burning so hot and
high that the firelight from down below poured upward
and inward, through the window of their hideout, to
dance wickedly on the ceiling.

"I will HUNT you down, boy!" thundered the
dragon Furious. "I smell your rotten human blood!
NOWHERE is safe for you! No cave, no rock, no
island. I shall turn this whole world into ashes thrice
over in the hunt for you...You can hide all you like.
You cannot hide forever...All it takes is one mistake
and...

## ...I SHALL HUNT YOU DOWN IN THE END!"

Oh yes, it was hard not to remain wakeful while
that destructive roar exploded in your ears like one
of Thor's worst thunderstorms, and the world burned
outside.

How were they ever going to get out of there, to
find the rest of the things and Camicazi?

From the sound of it, the dragon Furious was *never* going to give up.

After a while of everyone tossing and turning, the Wodensfang's wheezy voice cut through the darkness and the terrible noise.

"As no one is sleeping," said the Wodensfang, "allow me to tell you a story about a boy from the past who reminds me of this boy Snotlout here."

"Wodensfang!" said Hiccup, sitting bolt upright in surprise. "You're speaking Norse! I didn't know you could speak Norse! I thought it was only Stormfly here who had that gift."

"So did I," said Stormfly sadly. It was a bad night for Stormfly. Her mistress had gone missing, and now there was this revelation that somebody else shared her unique gift.

"Why have you never spoken Norse before, Wodensfang?" asked Hiccup.

"Just because you have a gift, it doesn't mean you need to tell everyone about it," replied the

Wodensfang simply. "I think the boy Snotlout might be interested in this…"

And in the darkness, the Wodensfang told the story of how the Dragonmark became the Slavemark.

Nobody could go to sleep. Nobody, that is, apart from the HOGFLY.

# HOW THE
# DRAGONMARK
## TURNED INTO THE

# SLAVEMARK

"Once upon a time," said the Wodensfang, "I was not the wrinkled little thing that you see before you now. You see," explained the Wodensfang, "I am a Sea-Dragon…"

Hiccup gasped. "YOU??? A Seadragonus Giganticus Maximus???"

"That's s-s-silly!" squeaked Toothless. "You're even smaller than T-t-toothless! How can you possibly be a Sea-Dragon?"

"There are many silly things that turn out to be true, Toothless," said the Wodensfang, smiling.

"Sea-Dragons start out small," the Wodensfang continued in Norse, "but they grow to immense size, like the fat full moon. And then they wane again…

"Once upon a time, Hiccup, a thousand or so years ago, when I was young and about the size of a Saber-Toothed Driver Dragon, I met your ancestor, Hiccup Horrendous Haddock the First, and I gave him the Dragon Jewel and trusted him with the Jewel's Secret."

"You told me this," said Hiccup.

"I did," said the Wodensfang. "I told you how Hiccup the First used the Secret of the Jewel to gain power over dragons and train them.

"But what I did not tell you was that in return for the Secret, Hiccup the First put a Mark upon himself.

"He put a Mark upon himself on the side of his forehead. It was a Mark in the shape of a dragon made out of his blood and the blood of his dragon brother. *My* blood. The Mark was the symbol of a promise, that the two of us were brothers, that we thought as one, that we would die for each other.

"As symbols will, it also became the symbol of the Kingdom of the Wilderwest. All the Warriors wore the symbol, blazing on their foreheads, so they were known as the Dragon-Riders.

"The Mark was known as the Dragonmark."

The young humans in the cave gasped in amazement.

"So the Mark was originally called the Dragonmark in the first place!" exclaimed Fishlegs.

Snotlout was very still, but his eyes were open. He was listening.

Hiccup touched the Mark, blazing purple on his forehead.

"So the first Dragonmark," Hiccup whispered, "was made out of your blood, Wodensfang?"

The Wodensfang nodded.

"For over a thousand years, it seemed like I had made the right decision to entrust the Secret of the Jewel to the humans. The Kingdom of the Wilderwest was a place of peace and prosperity in which dragons and humans lived in harmony with one another. The Secret was passed down from generation to generation, and its power was not abused. I grew huge as a mountainside, so large and splendid that I had to live in the ocean for a while.

"Ah…It was a golden age…" sighed the Wodensfang.

"Even as I began to shrink into my old age, many hundreds of years ago, I was still content that I had founded a new dynasty, a dynasty of happiness that would last forever…And then…"

"And then?" Hiccup whispered.

"And then, it seemed like I might have made a mistake in entrusting the Secret of the Dragon Jewel to the humans after all. You see, not all humans are as good as Hiccup the First.

"About a century ago, when I had shrunk to the size of a Viking hunting dog, a new King inherited the Throne. He was too young, really…about your age.

"His name was Speedfast," said the Wodensfang.

"Speedfast was not a bad character as a boy, but he was quick of temper and he had a tendency to bully his inferiors.

"This is the boy who reminds me so much of Snotlout here. He even looks like him. Like Snotlout, this boy refused to take the Dragonmark when he came of age.

" 'A King is brother to no man or dragon,' said the boy arrogantly. 'The *dragons* shall take the Mark, to show loyalty to their King, but *I* shall not take it.'

"That was all it took.

"The Mark that had been the symbol of brotherhood between man and dragon became a symbol of enslavement.

"For where the King went, his followers went too. The Boy Warrior, the future of their Tribe, refused to take the Mark, and in time the older generation became ashamed of the tattoo that had been a source of such pride and wore their helmets low upon their foreheads.

"And so it was with everything else. One by one, all the achievements of Hiccup the First were spoiled and ruined.

"And I...well, looking back, I do not think that I helped matters.

"For I *did* judge Speedfast harshly, then and now.

"I nagged him constantly about what he was doing. I told him he was betraying the memory of his ancestors. I scolded him, morning, noon and night.

"There is one particular time that I remember.

"Speedfast was sleeping in the King's bed. No one was supposed to disturb him. But I did not follow those rules. Why should I? I was his great-great-great-great-great-great-great-great-great-great-grandfather's blood brother.

"I flew in the window, perched on the headboard, and waited for him to wake.

"He opened his eyes, and there I was, stern and grave.

"'Why are you here?' said Speedfast, yawning, his handsome face instantly resentful.

"He spoke in Dragonese, the language he had learned since babyhood.

*tick
tock
tick
tock*

" 'You know why I am here,' I said gravely. 'You refuse to take the Mark. You use the Secret, entrusted to your father, to enslave my dragon brothers. You have just passed a law making slavery of humans legal again. You mark them with the Mark, which you now call the Slavemark.

" 'Your ancestors spent their lives building the Kingdom of the Wilderwest. Are you to throw that all away? You are betraying the work of men greater than you are...'

"The boy's face was as red as his hair.

" 'And *I* shall be a greater man than my ancestors ever were!' Speedfast shouted back at me. 'How dare you talk to me of betrayal! I shall make this tiny Kingdom of the Wilderwest a truly great empire, one that stretches to the very edges of the Rus to the east and down to the borders of Rome in the south. I will retake the land that my ancestors lost when that cursed Hiccup the First was born, the rich farmlands of the east, rather than these rocky island nothings.

" 'Even now I am building a great city on the island of Tomorrow, a city that shall rival Rome in glory and in power. But for that I need slave-power, dragon slaves and human slaves. So do not talk to me of betrayal! Tomorrow shall prove what a truly great King I shall be.'

"I scolded him again, too harshly perhaps. I said that he would never be as great a man as his ancestors, and a lot of other stern and severe things.

"Speedfast put his hands over his ears. 'Silence!' he screamed. 'I am banning the speaking of your devil language, Dragonese! Then I will not have to hear your forked-tongue nagging speech ever again!'

"That was the last time I saw the boy cry.

"He turned the Secret of the Jewel on me, told me to be gone or he would destroy all the dragons, banished me from his kingdom.

"And he was true to his word.

"The new Boy King banned the speaking of Dragonese. He shut his ancestors' library. He built a great city on the island of Tomorrow, a city of a hundred castles. The boy who was once Speedfast became the most feared Viking of all time, striking terror as far as the edges of the Rus and the borders of Rome."

HISTORY REPEATS ITSELF

Silence in the underground tree house, as everyone realized who this Speedfast must be.

"The boy who was once Speedfast?" asked Hiccup. He knew the answer even as he asked the question.

"He changed his name," said the dragon. "He changed his name to…"

"Grimbeard the Ghastly," finished Hiccup.

There was a long, long pause.

Hiccup felt slightly sick.

"Grimbeard the Ghastly. And as is often the way of these things, the gods set out to punish Grimbeard. Grimbeard had his own son, who was a runt, and also called Hiccup, Hiccup the Second. Grimbeard learned to love this son the best of all his children, but was tricked into killing his son because he thought he was stirring up a dragon rebellion against him. It was only then that he realized what a terrible mistake he had made, how he had betrayed both his own ancestors and his own son.

"That was why Grimbeard hid the things. He threw them to all quarters of the Archipelago so that only a true Hero could find them. A new King must be worthy. He set up a terrible bodyguard of almost superhuman Warriors and otherworldly dragons, to ensure that only a Hero with the ten Lost Things can be crowned King, and these dreadful bodyguards are known as the Guardian Protectors of Tomorrow."

Hiccup shivered. "I have heard bad things about those Guardians."

The Wodensfang nodded. "Yes, they must be terrible indeed, to have guarded Tomorrow for so many years.

"The Guardian Protectors of Tomorrow pass the Secret of the Dragon Jewel on from generation to generation.

"Only the Hero with the ten Lost Things can be crowned the King and live. Only he or she can be told the Secret.

"But that Hero must be worthy."

"Why are you telling us this?" said Hiccup.

"It's just a story," said the Wodensfang, "so that Snotlout can realize that the Slavemark was not always the Slavemark.

"And how quickly good things can be lost.

"And how a boy can change from being Speedfast to being Grimbeard the Ghastly...

"...And also the other way around."

Silence.

"Can somebody tell that ancient old dragon to SHUT UP?" said Snotlout rudely. "I'm TRYING to sleep."

Silence in the cave again.

One by one, the exhausted humans and dragons fell asleep, despite the noise from outside, despite their fears for Camicazi.

But Hiccup remained awake, tossing and turning and worrying, about Camicazi, about the rebellion, about whether Snotlout was a traitor...

These were the last thoughts he had before he drifted off to sleep.

Much later, Snotlout awoke. He reached into his ragged breast pocket, behind his armor, and drew out a Black Star.

Snotlout had won that star for outstanding bravery in the Battle of the Lucky Thirteen* years ago, when Snotlout and Hiccup first met Alvin the Treacherous. Gobber the Belch, his old teacher, had told Snotlout it was one of the

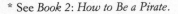

* See *Book 2: How to Be a Pirate*.

proudest days of his life, to see a pupil of his win such an honor.

Snotlout's face was expressionless as he looked at the star.

The Deadly Shadow, who happened to be awake at that hour, let out a small warning growl, just to let Snotlout know that he was being watched.

Snotlout put the Black Star back in his pocket and turned over so that the dragon could not see his face.

Snotlout was crying.

# 7. TOOTHLESS'S DREAM

Much, MUCH later that night, Toothless had a terrifying dream.

It was terrifying because it felt so real. He dreamed he woke up, and in front of him was the underground tree house where they were sleeping—but at the same time it was not quite the tree house. It merged into somewhere else, in that way of dreams, and that somewhere was very cold.

The Wodensfang was awake too and staring straight in front of him. His eyes had turned a very strange sort of purple color. The scar on his chest almost seemed to be glowing. Toothless had a scar too, in almost exactly the same place, and it suddenly itched and burned as if he had received it yesterday.

And there in the tree house, very loud, was the sound of a voice Toothless recognized. It was the voice of the dragon Furious.

Toothless lay still, trembling.

Toothless could hear the roaring of the dragon rebellion *outside*, screaming and raging at full catastrophic force. But, to Toothless's absolute terror, it sounded as if the voice of the dragon Furious was coming from *inside* the tree house. But how was that possible? The dragon Furious wasn't there, and he was too big to fit inside.

Maybe he had lifted up the mountaintop and was looking down at them from above?

Rigid with anxiety, Toothless slowly, slowly tipped his head upward.

No, the ceiling was still there. Phew.

So where on earth was the voice coming from? It was a mystery.

"TRAITOR!" roared the dragon Furious. "TRAITOR!"

For one heart-stopping moment Toothless feared the dragon Furious was talking to *him*, and he gave an unhappy whine and hid his head in his paws. But no. The dragon Furious was talking to the Wodensfang.

"Why are you letting my thoughts in now, Wodensfang?" screamed the dragon Furious, in an apocalyptic rage. "Have you changed your mind about your treacherous behavior? Are you ashamed of betraying your dragonhood for the second time?"

The voice of the
Wodensfang replied. Both the
Wodensfang and the dragon Furious
were speaking in Norse, not Dragonese.
But the Wodensfang, though awake, did
not move his lips. How was that possible?

"Now, now, Furious," replied the
Wodensfang. "Calm down. This anger is
exhausting you. And do not be so quick to
think I am betraying us."

The dragon Furious quieted his
rage for a moment, but his tone was
still bitterly resentful. "You are a
Seadragonus Giganticus Maximus,
Wodensfang, and a very old one. So you
can see into the future even better than
I can. You know that the boy will be the
end of us all, if we let him live."

The Wodensfang sighed. He did
not contradict the dragon Furious.

"BUT I WILL NOT LET THAT
HAPPEN!" roared the dragon
Furious. "I have pledged that Hiccup
the Third shall not reach Tomorrow.
And he is near—I sense it. I

smell you both in my heart, although you are protecting him. I will not give up. I will stay here until I hunt you out, however long that takes."

The dragon paused in his rage for a moment and tried to reason with the Wodensfang.

"There is no time anymore for the foolish hopes of a silly old dragon. Do you think you are the only one who has ever loved a human? I loved one once myself. His name was Hiccup the Second. But in the end, these Hiccup boys, wonderful as they are, will not be able to defeat the strength of the evil that runs through humanity. Look how the kingdom of Hiccup the First fell into the hands of the boy who was once Speedfast and ended up Grimbeard the Ghastly. And see how this boy, Hiccup the Third, finds the Lost Things, and they fall again and again into the hook of the evil one, Alvin the Treacherous."

The Wodensfang sighed. "That

has been worrying me, I confess."

"Fate is trying to tell you something, Wodensfang. We have to learn from the past, as well as the future."

The Wodensfang sat still, looking into the future.

"You are mistaken if you think this has not occurred to me," said the Wodensfang, almost as if he were talking to himself. "In part, I am doing this because I want to believe in the impossible, and young humans are so touching in their belief in the impossible."

"When we are old, we must be wise and give up what is unrealistic," said the dragon Furious. "You had the chance to kill the boy in the Fire Cavern. You could not do it, so bring the boy to someone who CAN do it. I will kill him for the sake of all of us. I am the King of the Dragons, and a King has to act for the greater good."

"That is the way the witch talks," said the Wodensfang softly.

"You may love humans, but you are, in the end, a dragon. You have to put your dragonhood first. Bring the boy to me, as you know you must," said the dragon Furious. "Furthermore, you know you will."

The Wodensfang sat silent for a long time. Toothless had the impression that he was playing some game of chess with the possibilities in his mind. Eventually the Wodensfang said, "All right, Furious. I will betray whoever is made King."

Toothless stiffened in horror.

"But not yet," said the Wodensfang. "I want this story to play out to the very final moment. I want the boy to have the chance to be the biggest Hero he can be before the story ends where it must…"

All right, Furious.
I will betray the King.

"He is so close now, to being a Hero.
I do not want to bring him down before he
makes it there. Once I helped a boy become
a King. Let me do this one more time before I
die, for this one human, even if it ends in the
destruction of a species. I will make you a
bargain. Stop stalking us. Call off your hunt,
take your dragon rebellion north to prepare
for the war on Tomorrow…"

"Why would I do that?" scorned
Furious. "I am close to you now. I feel it."

"But you are wasting your strength
in these angry attacks," the Wodensfang
pointed out, "and you need to save it
for the final battle. You are frightened of
Tomorrow; you fear it, Furious, do you not?
So go back north and prepare. The twelfth day
of Doomsday is only two days away, and you
need to be at full strength.

"This way, *you* get a little breathing
space, and *I* get some last

No!

precious hours with the boy," wheezed the Wodensfang with a deep and longing melancholy.

The dragon Furious considered this.

"If I were to give you this time," growled the dragon Furious, "if I were to halt my rebellion, only to strike with greater strength on the day of Doomsday of Yule itself, what would *you* offer me in return?"

"I would swear to you, by the word of a Sea-Dragon," said the Wodensfang, "that if a King is crowned on the Doomsday of Yule, on that very same day, I will bring that King to meet you in single combat."

The dragon Furious grunted. "That is no use to me, if the King is carrying the jewel."

"But *before* the King rides out to meet you," said the Wodensfang, "I shall take the Dragon Jewel from them, and bring it to you."

The dragon Furious growled in satisfaction.

"So this puny human King will be forced to meet *me*, the dragon Furious, in single combat with no Jewel to protect them?"

"That is correct," said the Wodensfang,

"I TAKE YOUR BARGAIN!" cried the dragon Furious, and Toothless jumped to hear the thunderclap of his jubilation.

"Swear you will bring the jewel to me, and then the King," said the dragon Furious sternly.

"I swear on the word of a Sea-Dragon that I shall bring them both to you," said the Wodensfang, sighing miserably. "But it is a bitter bargain."

"No!" shrieked Toothless in his thoughts. "The word of a Sea-Dragon cannot be broken. No! No! No! No! No!"

"And I swear that I will call off the hunt in return." said the dragon Furious. "You are right. I confess that this anger is exhausting. It will be good to rest for the final conflict.

"Dragons of the rebellion!" called the mighty beast. "HALT THE RED-RAGE!"

And Toothless could hear the sound of the dragon rebellion outside quieting down.

Then the Wodensfang smiled. "And now at least you can stop tracking us, Furious, through the thoughts of the gummy one, and I can stop blocking you, which will be more relaxing for both of us…"

The dragon Furious laughed. "Such thoughts as they are! I can't believe *he's* a Seadragonus Giganticus Maximus, the little stammering toothless one! He's so stupid, and he seems to think of nothing but food!"

"He's just young," scolded the Wodensfang. "He doesn't yet know what he is…"

"Here, I s-s-say!" protested Toothless, and he was so distressed he spoke aloud. "You're n-n-not talking about Toothless, are you? How can Toothless be a Sea-Dragon? That's even s-s-sillier than the *Wodensfang* being one! Toothless doesn't want d-d-dragons listening into his thoughts! And Toothless does know what he is! He's a Common-or-Gar—actually, no, he's a Toothless Daydream…

"Well, whatever he is, Toothless N-N-NOT a Sea-Dragon. He's far too small—this is a very bad dream!"

The Wodensfang turned his head toward Toothless. "That's right, it is a very bad dream, Toothless,"

said the
voice of the
Wodensfang,
still without
opening his mouth but
looking straight at Toothless
with his hypnotic eyes. "But
you can go back to sleep now,
and when you wake up, you will
have forgotten all about it…"

"A very bad dream," said the
fading voice of the dragon Furious.

Toothless yawned.

Slowly he closed his eyes and
went back to sleep.

When he woke up in the morning, he shivered.

The sound of the dragon rebellion outside had gone.

That was a VERY bad dream he'd had last night.

But what was it about?

He couldn't remember for the life of him.

That was a VERY bad dream...

Meanwhile...

Somewhere in the darkness, Camicazi was crying, even though Bog-Burglars DO NOT cry.

And in a greater darkness still, a pair of floating red eyes were moving slo-o-owly, inexorably toward Hiccup...

"My tooth... Whe-e-ere is my tooth? When I find the horrid little boy who has my good tooth, I shall <u>kill</u> him. Whe-e-ere is my tooth?"

# 8. YOU WOULDN'T FIND ALVIN'S SECRET CAMP EVEN IF YOU SEARCHED FOR A HUNDRED YEARS

The next morning, to Hiccup's surprise, the dragons of the dragon rebellion had vanished. Outside, the landscape was a smoking, burning ruin, but there was no sign of human or dragon life. The rain poured down relentlessly.

"They've gone…" breathed Hiccup, unable to believe their good fortune. "Now we can go and

"FOLLOW ME," said Hiccup.

"We HAVE to find Camicazi, whatever the risk..."

rescue Camicazi."

"Do you think that this is a trick?" whispered Fishlegs. "Surely we will still be ambushed on our way to Alvin's camp?"

"I have a sense that we will be fine," wheezed the Wodensfang, in Norse. "Don't ask me *how* I know, but the dragon Furious will not attack us...*for now*."

But even with the Wodensfang's reassurance, it was terrifying to venture out of the hideout once again, with the worry that at any moment they might be attacked by the dragon Furious, or by the witch's Spydragons.

The tree above the underground tree house was still burning when they left it, a blackened, smoldering stump.

Snotlout, on the back of the Hurricane, led them through the eerie landscape. Hiccup had seen woods destroyed before, but this was ten times worse. Everyone was silent, awed by the devastation.

What had once been the half-burned remains of a forest now looked like the smoking surface of the moon. If it hadn't been for the river, they would never have found their way, for the landscape was unrecognizable.

Whole mountains had been demolished, shaken to rubble as if there had been an earthquake, whole forests reduced to little toasted sticks of kindling and ash.

Every now and then the river itself was blocked and dammed by gigantic torn-up rocks from an obliterated hillside. Water spurted up and around the obstructions like blood from a wound before reverting to its original course.

The bite in Hiccup's arm was a constant reminder of the Vampire Spydragon. It could track him down through the tooth still buried in his flesh. It could appear out of nowhere, out of nothing, so Hiccup was constantly looking over his shoulder, feeling that at any moment he could be attacked once again.

The bruise had spread so that the whole of the left side of Hiccup's body was purple, right down to his knee.

"I look like a Mood Dragon!" Hiccup joked, but that was to cover up how frightened he was.

All the discolored areas were so numb that he couldn't feel or use his left arm at all. It was hard

"We WILL find her...
We WILL..."

to cling on to the Deadly Shadow's back. He told himself that the Spydragon had been scared off by the scale of the dragon rebellion attack last night, along with everything else. They crept through the devastation, scurrying, terrified, to hide behind the corpse of one blasted tree, and then on to another, and even though they were shaded by the wings of the Deadly Shadow, they felt painfully visible—the only moving things in a wasteland of nothing.

*This must be what it is like at the end of the world*, thought Hiccup.

"Wow," breathed Snotlout. "That dragon really *does* want to get you, doesn't he, Useless? I wouldn't want to be in your shoes if he ever finds you…"

"But why isn't the dragon Furious *here*?" muttered Hiccup, the tic in his eye working as he squinted all around them. "Why isn't he stalking us? He knows we are in these mountains, somewhere. Why is he not hunting? That isn't like a dragon. It doesn't feel right.

When a dragon has something trapped, it goes in for
the kill. Where has he gone?"

The Wodensfang fluttered innocently above
Hiccup's head.

Out of nowhere, Toothless suddenly bit him.

"OW! Toothless! That isn't nice!" said Hiccup.
"Not good manners at all..."

"S-s-sorry," whimpered Toothless, thoroughly
bewildered. "Not sure why Toothless did that...Is all
a bit scary for poor Toothless..."

Rattled and jumpy,
Toothless was indeed not
quite himself.

They made their way down
the river and dismounted from their
dragons beside the gigantic sea cliff
waterfall where Camicazi and Snotlout
had nearly fallen to their deaths the
previous night.

"Alvin's camp is right *here*," announced Snotlout
proudly. "It's colossal. Hundreds and hundreds of
boats, and a whole floating town."

"What on earth do you mean?" asked Fishlegs,
shielding his eyes and peering out to sea. "Is this camp
invisible, like the Vampire Spydragons?"

Fishlegs had a point. In front of them, as far as
the eye could see, was a desolate ocean wasteland,
punctuated by monumental icebergs in fantastical
ghost shapes.

There was no sign at all of an enormous hidden
camp.

"I mean exactly what I say, Fish-eggs," said
Snotlout. "*Here* is Alvin's camp."

Hiccup and Fishlegs looked at Snotlout with
open mouths.

"Are you mad? Or just
lying?" asked Fishlegs. "A camp can't
be invisible!"

"That's why you need *me*," said Snotlout
smugly. "It's right underneath us."

He paused for effect.

"The camp is behind the waterfall."

The humans and the dragons looked at him with
round, amazed eyes.

"Behind this waterfall is a truly immense sea
cavern," boasted Snotlout. "Inside that cavern, on stilts
over the water, the witch and Alvin have built their war
bunker."

Hiccup and Fishlegs looked in awe at the
tremendous cascade of water, falling down, down,
down into the sea below.

"Well, I'll be hornswoggled," breathed the Wodensfang. "No wonder Stoick and Valhallarama haven't found this camp…"

Hiccup swallowed. "So what's the plan, Snotlout? You know the territory. How do we get behind this waterfall? And once we're there, how do we steal the Lost Things and rescue Camicazi?"

"Nice to see you're putting me in charge for once, Useless," drawled Snotlout. "Listen and learn, Hiccup, and you'll see how a real leader plans a military operation…

"Now," he said briskly, "flying behind the waterfall is quite easy. In the center of the waterfall, the water is an impenetrable force that would sweep you down and smash you on the rocks below. But at the edges, the fall is quite light, and you can fly right through it."

"Ingenious," said Hiccup, impressed at his enemy's cleverness in spite of himself.

"But once we're actually *in* the cavern, things get dangerous."

"Oh, no…" Toothless shivered. "Toothless h-h-hates it when it's dangerous."

"The cavern is patrolled day and night by Alvinsmen sentries, on foot and on the back of

Bullguards. We'll have to fly inside, in formation, with the Windwalker and the Hurricane flying low under the Deadly Shadow so that hopefully the sentries won't spot them…"

"H-h-hopefully…" groaned Toothless. "Toothless hates 'hopefully'…"

"The underground village is built on wooden platforms over the water. So we'll head straight for those wooden platforms and fly underneath them.

"There are hatches along the way where the Alvinsmen throw garbage down and catch fish. I can take us to the hatch that leads up into the room where they are keeping the Lost Things. We'll sneak in, steal the things, and load them onto the Deadly Shadow's back through the hatch."

"This is a ridiculous plan!" howled Fishlegs. "I can't believe you're even thinking about it, Hiccup!"

"Your fishlegged friend is suspicious, Hiccup…" said Snotlout, his eyes glinting. "The question is, are you?"

"I'm going to trust you," said Hiccup.

"Oh frizzling fuzzy fish-fingers of Loki," moaned Fishlegs, to no one in particular. "All I wanted was a nice, quiet life as a *bard*. A little cottage. A nice lyre. It's not much to ask, is it? But what do the gods make me instead? A major contestant in an interspecies WAR. I mean, I ask you, talk about bad luck…"

The Windwalker huddled next to Fishlegs and gave him an affectionate and understanding lick on the face. Fishlegs grinned in spite of himself. "Dragon slobber. Always makes everything better."

"Excellent," said Snotlout, climbing astride the Hurricane. "Follow closely behind me."

Snotlout took off, but before the others could follow, Hiccup motioned them into a huddle.

"What are we doing?" whispered Fishlegs.

"I *want* to trust Snotlout," said Hiccup. "I really, really *want* to trust him, but I am not quite sure that we can. So in case he does happen to betray us after all, here is Plan B."

"Ah," murmured the Wodensfang. "That is wise. You are learning, Hiccup. Hope for the best, but at the same time prepare for the worst. That is kingly behavior."

Fishlegs agreed. "Oh phew, I'm so glad there is a Plan B. I'm not very keen on Plan A."

As quick as he could, Hiccup outlined Plan B to everyone, and both dragons and humans nodded to say they understood.

"But Plan B is even more dangerous than Plan A!" complained Fishlegs.

"Well, I'm really hoping we won't have to put it into action," said Hiccup grimly.

"COME ON!" Snotlout whispered from where he was hovering about thirty feet below, at the edges of the waterfall. "We haven't got all night, scaredy-cats! *I'm* the leader now, and when I say go, GO! Honestly, Hiccup, you and your sidekicks have no idea of military obedience, no idea at all..."

"I like this New Improved Snotlout, with Added Old-Fashioned Charm," said Fishlegs, climbing aboard the Deadly Shadow. "Don't you?"

Hiccup rode the Windwalker, and Fishlegs the Deadly Shadow. They hovered for a moment or two on the edge of the waterfall, getting into position.

Looking at the tumultuous cascade in front of them, it seemed impossible that there could be anything on the other side.

"You have to fly through it quite fast, so get a bit of speed up," advised Snotlout. "Ready? NOW!"

Fishlegs went first.

He gave a few gentle taps with his heels. The Deadly Shadow reared upward in alarm, for it was as if

Fishlegs was driving straight at a wall of water. But the three heads put their mouths in a determined line, and the great chameleon dragon turned itself exactly the color of falling water and flew straight at the cascade at considerable speed.

It was a peculiar feeling plunging through the waterfall.

An instant's soaking, chilling stun of water, so cold that they nearly screamed—and Toothless, flying above, did indeed let out an unhappy squeak—and then they were out the other side, gasping with the shock of it. Fishlegs braked the Deadly Shadow sharply, and the dragon reared up to hide the Windwalker and the Hurricane hurtling in after them.

WHAT a sight greeted their blinking, drenched eyes.

# 9. INSIDE ALVIN'S WAR BUNKER

It was a stupendous underground ice cavern, titanically huge, and lit with millions and millions of glowworms that sent the ice gleaming and dazzling as the glowworms moved. There were vast icicles hanging down from the ceiling, as if something had exploded from above and frozen into great spikes of turquoise ice.

The floor of the cavern was sea, and above it, as Snotlout had said, the witch and Alvin had built a Viking town on stilts. A crazy maze of wooden platforms wound nearly from one side of the cavern to the other, with houses and blacksmiths' forges and armories and even a crooked Great Hall standing in the center, made out of what looked like the jumbled remains of ships, with the skull-and-crossbones Treacherous flag flying from the top.

At the edges of this town there were at least a hundred black ships, skulking like predatory black widow spiders, torches and flares glowing along their sides. And there was a melancholy, familiar sight of gigantic dragon cages, with that terrible sound of captured, terrified dragons, and the smell of chains being made out of molten metal, for Alvin and the witch were using dragons as slaves again.

It was good for Hiccup to see this at this time, for it was so easy, in the chaos and the horror of war, to forget what they were fighting for. It reminded Hiccup that though he had made mistakes—he had released the dragon Furious, he had lost Camicazi—he had made those mistakes for a reason.

This must not happen.

This misery, this slavery, this must not happen in the future.

A new world HAD to be born.

With a sick feeling in his stomach, Hiccup recognized Dragonmarker helmets on long poles sticking triumphantly above the town.

Poor Camicazi was in there somewhere.

*Oh please let her be all right...*

Ferocious-looking Alvinsmen Warriors hurried along the wooden walkways, shouting at one another, and lighting flares and cooking food and making weapons.

Circling above were the Alvinsmen sentries, riding Bullguard Slavedragons whose goggling eyes sent out searchlight beams as they patrolled the camp, guarding against intruders.

It was extraordinary to think that such a huge gathering of houses and ships could have been hidden from the Dragonmarkers and the dragon Furious for so long, but the roar of the waterfall had entirely muffled the noises and the smells and the lights of this busy underground town from outside.

Hiccup adjusted his sword.

"Let's go," he whispered.

The three-headed dragon swooped down toward the wooden platforms of the bustling village, the Windwalker and the Hurricane flying low under the Deadly Shadow's wings, so that they would be camouflaged as they passed through the circling Bullguard sentries.

Snotlout's eyes gleamed admiringly as the beautiful Deadly Shadow dragon plunged into a dive.

"I have to admit, reluctantly, Useless," he whispered, "that for a lot of runty little weeds, your team does travel in style."

Hiccup's heart was beating so hard it felt as if it might leap out of his chest at any moment as they soared near the Bullguards. One of the Bullguards whipped its head around, perhaps feeling the passing wind from the Deadly Shadow's wings or hearing the little muffled whispers of the hunting dragons…

*Surely they must see us?* thought Hiccup, petrified.

They swooped downward, and Hiccup tipped his face upward, expecting at any minute a roar of discovery and then the whine of a full aerial pursuit. But there was nothing, no suspicion in the faces of the Alvinsmen sentries or the dragons they were riding. The Bullguards continued their patrol, their eye beams flashing around the bay in steady circles.

Down the Deadly Shadow swooped and shot underneath the nearest wooden platform, followed by the Hurricane and the Windwalker, and the Hogfly, Stormfly, the Wodensfang, and Toothless.

Hiccup breathed a sigh of relief.

There was barely room for the Deadly Shadow underneath the maze of wooden platforms. Its wings dipped into the sea as it flew, swerving through the stilts that stood in the water like legs.

It was bizarre to be flying *underneath* the streets of a city. Looking up, in between the wooden boards, Hiccup could see the shoes of people walking up and down the walkways above. A hatch opened ahead of them, and the Windwalker swerved just in time, for someone chucked a bucket of fish guts through the hatch before slamming it shut again.

Below them in the water were the rotting

carcasses of sunken ships. Snotlout landed the Hurricane on the upturned hull of one of these submerged wrecks and gestured upward with his thumb.

"This is the hatch," he whispered. "Before the witch caught us, the Hurricane and I went on loads of spying operations searching for the things. Look, I've marked the hatch with an *X*, to be sure I'd get the right one when I came back."

Hiccup and Fishlegs landed their dragons beside him, and the three dragons sat in a row on the hull of the sunken ship, like three great cormorants roosting on a rock.

"And who is in there guarding them?"

Snotlout's eyes gleamed.

"Oh, a couple of dozing Alvinsmen guards. But we can deal with them, can't we?"

"He lies..." whispered Stormfly in Dragonese. "Trust a liar to know a liar..."

"If all three of us climb up," said Snotlout, "we can carry the Throne through the hatch and balance it on the back of the Deadly Shadow. And then we'll go on to the prison and rescue Camicazi."

Hiccup drew his sword and swallowed hard.

"Okay," said Hiccup. "Wodensfang, Hogfly,

and Stormfly, you stay here with the Windwalker and the Deadly Shadow."

"Woof, woof!" said the Hogfly obediently. "Keep to the left! Marry me, sunshine! Where's the exit?"

"Toothless," said Hiccup, "you can come with me. I don't want to let you out of my sight..."

"Because T-t-toothless is the best Lost Thing?" Toothless smiled radiantly. "See, Stormfly...See, W-w-wodensfang...See, very, very stupid dragon who looks like a pig...Toothless so important Hiccup can't let him out of his sight...Toothless V-V-VERY VERY important..."

"The Deadly Shadow can give all three of us a lift up to the hatch. Windwalker, could you open it for us, please?" said Hiccup.

A single breath from the Windwalker incinerated the bolts around the hatch, and it fell open.

Hiccup, sitting on the back of the Deadly Shadow, who was hovering just underneath the hatch, peered up inside. It was completely dark, and completely quiet.

"I'll go in first," whispered Snotlout, "because I know my way around..."

Snotlout's eyes were curiously bright.

Was it excitement?

Or was it something more than that?

147

Snotlout laughed at Hiccup's expression, which was a little dubious. "You do trust me, don't you, Hiccup?"

"*T-t-toothless* doesn't trust him..." said Toothless's deep little voice from down in Hiccup's waistcoat. "Is like trusting a s-s-snake not to bite you..."

"I *want* to trust you," said Hiccup steadily. "I really really *want* to trust you, Snotlout..."

Snotlout dropped his own gaze. Did he look guilty, just for a fraction of a second?

Then he drew his dagger and put it between his teeth.

Snotlout stood up on the Deadly Shadow's back and hauled himself onto the ledge of the hatch, where he swung for a moment before climbing into the darkness above and disappearing.

"Is *m-m-madness*," said the muffled voice of Toothless.

It *was* madness. Snotlout hadn't really given Hiccup cause to trust him in the past.

But barely had Snotlout's feet disappeared through the hatch and into the room than Hiccup scrambled up after him.

Hiccup swallowed hard and got to his feet and tried to make out where Snotlout was.

"Snotlout?" he whispered nervously.

There was no answer.

The darkness was so absolute it muffled the senses. Hiccup's eyes peered desperately into the blackness, but he could see nothing.

"Snotlout?" he whispered again, a little louder, but again there was no reply, just a faint rustling.

Why was Snotlout being so silent? He must be in the room somewhere…He had only climbed through the hatch two seconds before Hiccup…

Hiccup automatically edged softly, softly backward, as he began to suspect what this silence might mean. And then a familiar smell reached his nostrils, a faint stink of rotting eggs…

Hiccup would have recognized that stench anywhere.

That delicate little aroma was the foul skunk smell of the Murderous Tribe, and every single member of the Murderous Tribe was a loyal Alvinsman servant of Alvin and the witch.

He could hear a shuffling of immense feet,

and a hoarse breathing of not just one great Warrior, but many.

It only meant one thing.

BETRAYAL.

TREACHERY AND BETRAYAL.

Snotlout had betrayed him.

Down in the depths of Hiccup's waistcoat, Toothless was giving Hiccup gentle, desperate nips on the tummy.

*I should run!* thought Hiccup. *Drop back through that hatch and fly away on the back of the Windwalker!*

But if Snotlout had betrayed him, it meant that Snotlout did not really know where the Lost Things were hidden. So there was only one thing left to do.

It was time to put Plan B into action.

Hiccup thrust his head down through the hatch. Fishlegs was already standing on the Deadly Shadow's back, screwing up his courage to squirm up behind Hiccup.

"Plan B!" whispered Hiccup.

Fishlegs looked back at him with shocked eyes.

"No...not Plan B...Has Snotlout betrayed us already?"

"Plan B!" Hiccup repeated.

And then Hiccup ignored all those instincts

screaming at him to run away and moved away from the hatch, from escape and freedom, back into the unknown of the darkened room.

Two more steps and Hiccup was grabbed by rough hands.

"GOT HIM!" yelled the Alvinsman, and three more Warriors seized Hiccup as well, punching him, hitting him, even though Hiccup put up no resistance.

From darkness he was hauled into dazzling light, into a room full of chattering people. The noise died away as soon as he was dragged in.

Blinded by the light, Hiccup recognized the person who spoke next from the sound of his voice.

It was strangely changed, that voice, muffled and disfigured into a ghastly, shrieking rasp. But nonetheless, it was definitely the voice of Hiccup's greatest enemy, Alvin the Treacherous.

"Why, HICCUP HORRENDOUS HADDOCK THE THIRD, as I live and breathe! Thank you so much for joining us…"

# Winterfleshers

## ~ STATISTICS ~

**FEAR FACTOR:** ......................... 6
**ATTACK:** ................................. 7
**SPEED:** .................................. 5
**SIZE:** .................................... 2
**DISOBEDIENCE:** ..................... 7

Winterfleshers are small dragons and, with their mouths shut look quite sweet, but actually they are a little like piranhas. When they attack in shoals they can strip a deer down to its skeleton in precisely three minutes.

SNAP!

SNAP!

SNAP!

# 10. TREACHERY AND BETRAYAL

As his eyes grew accustomed to the light, Hiccup realized he must be in the crooked Great Hall, right in the center of the floating town. This assembly room was crudely fashioned out of the upturned hulls of three ancient Viking ships that had once been sunk by the reefs of Wrecker's Bay.

Around the edges of the room were cages containing human and dragon prisoners, stacked on top of one another, right up to the ceiling.

In the middle of the hall stood the Alvinsmen.

The Alvinsmen were a grim, tattooed, unsightly crew of vicious and murderous criminals who had once been the more unpleasant members of the Visithug, Murderous, Outcast, Hysteric, and Uglithug Tribes. The nastier side of the Archipelago had all followed Alvin and the witch, and had grown ghastlier as a result. It had brought out the worst in them.

The Alvinsmen dragged Hiccup into the center of the hall and pushed him forward, in front of a man in an iron mask.

Snotlout swaggered in afterward.

It took a few seconds for Hiccup to recognize

the man in the iron mask as Alvin
the Treacherous.

Alvin's mother had given Alvin
a nasty case of warts. As Alvin had
gained in power, so too had his warts:
multiplying, blossoming, and blooming
in mushrooming abundance. Big warts had
given birth to little warts, and those little
warts in their turn had grown and swelled and
had babies and burst across his face like
joyful volcanoes spewing pus, ripening and
germinating in such rosy profusion that
his face had swelled beyond all recognition.
What had begun as happy additions, spotty little
adornments to his beauty, had ended finally in
disfigurement.

So Alvin was wearing an iron mask to
hide his swollen face. Beneath the mask,
the warts had swollen up his lips as if
they had been
stung by
bees.

That, and the grill across his mouth, gave his breathing and his voice a dreadful rasping quality.

He was wearing none of the Lost Things...not even the ruby heart's stone bracelet.

Alvin was now a Man of War.

He was a Warrior made almost entirely out of metal, from his gleaming hook to the spears and swords and arrows hanging around his person. Even his ivory leg was capped in steel. Along with many other dreadful instruments of war suspended around his waist, he had not only Dragonmarker helmets, but the sad remnants of their beards.

On recognition of Hiccup, he let out a yell of delight that was distorted by the grill of the mask into a rasping animal screech.

The witch Excellinor bounded over on all fours.

She was a long, lean wolf skeleton with a terrible dead whiteness to her, bleached of all human kindness and color. She ought to have been a woman, but her semi-baldness and her tattoos and the long white hairs sprouting in a little beard on her jutting chin seemed to suggest something else.

In one bound she pinned Hiccup to the floor, a wild animal about to strike, and she opened up her terrible jaws with those sharklike teeth, ground and sharpened into points, and screamed so loudly that she showered poor Hiccup with her horrible witch spittle:

"WE'VE GOT HIM! WE'VE GOT HIM, THE LITTLE WRETCH! VICTORY IS OURS!"

Hiccup shrank away from her, for she was terrifying, and whatever dead animal she had been chewing on had stuck between her teeth and made her breath stink.

Great cheers went up from the Alvinsmen.

Groans from the Dragonmarker prisoners, held in the cages on the edges of the room.

The witch reared up on her hind legs, dragging Hiccup to his feet.

"Oh, well done, Snotlout, well done!" she caroled. "Well done, my poisonous boy! Hiccup believed you!"

We've GOT

*him* !!!

"He believed every
single subtle word,"
smirked Snotlout,
high-fiving the Alvinsmen
and even Alvin himself (which
was actually a slightly painful
experience, because Alvin had a
hook rather than a hand).

"Oh, this is excellent news," sang
Alvin. "It means I shall be eating Hiccup's
heart by this evening…"

"You're revolting!" snapped a voice.

It was coming from inside a large box in the
corner of the room.

"Camicazi!"

*Oh thank Thor and Woden and pretty much everybody.* Hiccup was quite limp with relief.

"Are you all right in there, Camicazi?"

"I'm fine!" said the voice from the box cheerfully. "I could not be finer. Don't you worry about me, Hiccup. I am absolutely okay…"

"Why have you put Camicazi in a box?" Hiccup demanded of the witch.

"I didn't want the little Escape Artist to escape…" purred the witch in reply.

The box was neatly wrapped up in heavy chains and padlocks.

*Camicazi!*
*I'm SORRY, Camicazi…*

The witch was taking absolutely no chances.

"Are you *sure* you're all right, Camicazi?" Hiccup shouted at the box. He hadn't forgotten her for a moment in all this time; how could he?

"Oh yes," said the box. "It's roomier in here than it looks, quite comfy really, and there are plenty of air holes. But 'eating his heart' indeed! You should be ashamed of yourself, Alvin! And you never learn, Witch! Hiccup will trick you again, just like he always does, and it'll be *you* who is checkmated, just like all the other times!"

"Poor little Bog-Burglar," cooed the witch. "The winds of war can change, my pretty love, the winds of war can change. Your boyfriend has a weakness, you see…"

"Hiccup is NOT my boyfriend!" protested the box furiously.

"He wants to believe the best of people," continued the witch, ignoring her. "And as a result, Snotlout seems to have tricked him pretty easily."

"That traitor!" spat the box.

"I expect you *warned* Hiccup not to trust Snotlout, didn't you, Camicazi?" purred the witch.

By the silence from the box, the witch knew she had scored a hit.

"Tut tut," soothed the witch. "You see, my pretty one? Kings must not be so easily tricked. Can you not see that you have backed the wrong side? The boy's father has *failed* to find our hideout; the boy's mother has *failed* to steal the Lost Things. The boy himself is so weak that he has walked straight into my trap. He isn't really the right stuff to be a King, is he?"

"*You are evil!*" shouted the voice of Camicazi from inside the box.

"Thank you," smiled the witch. "As I was saying, the winds of war can change in a heartbeat. And you too can change sides if you want. Everyone in this room should know that it's not too late to change your loyalties and be on the winning side."

" I will never Turn My Back on you again, Hiccup."

"NEVER!" cried Camicazi. "You can't see me, Hiccup, but inside this box, I am quite definitely NOT turning my back!"

"Why would you want to follow Hiccup? He's a fool!" screamed the witch. "The fool! The fool!

The fool! Believed the word of someone who has betrayed him twice before? How could he be such an idiot?"

"Because I know there is good in Snotlout," said Hiccup, stubbornly trying to cross his arms, but failing to do so because one of his arms was sort of floppy.

"Oh for Thor's sake, Hiccup," snapped Snotlout. "Stop forgiving me. It's *really* irritating."

"Snotlout, you are a TRAITOR!" came a bellow from a cage in the corner of the room.

It was Gobber the Belch, Hiccup's old teacher, who must have been captured by the Alvinsmen.

His magnificent golden yellow beard, a sign of his proud Warriorhood, had been hacked off at the roots. It was hard to look at his face now that it was edged with that rough, ragged desecration. That was the worst thing you could do to a

Gobber the Belch's magnificent yellow beard had been hacked off at the roots.

*I have your beard, old man!*

Viking Warrior. It was like hacking off a lion's mane.

Gobber's ex-beard was now hanging like a scalp from Alvin's waist, and Alvin ran it jeeringly through his fingers and shook it at Gobber tauntingly.

"I have your beard, old man," he chanted softly through his mask. "I have your beard."

But Gobber was alive, at least.

And still fighting.

"SNOTLOUT!" bellowed Gobber. "I offered you the chance to change sides back in the Slavelands. I said then that you would be an asset to the Company of the Dragonmark. I withdraw that offer. You are a disgrace to your name and your Tribe!"

Snotlout bit his lip. But he recovered to say contemptuously: "Well, at least I'm not locked up in a cage. Now that really would be a disgrace."

The Alvinsmen soldiers laughed uproariously at that.

"Better a noble slave than a free dog," shouted Gobber.

Snotlout flushed.

"*You* betrayed *me*," said Snotlout fiercely. "You betrayed everything you ever taught me about life. And look what has happened—look at the result of this weakness!" Snotlout gestured to the world outside. "The world at war! The dragons on the edge of destroying us all! And still you are saying that it is I who am the traitor? *You* are the traitor! You are all traitors to the world that I loved!"

"How dare you call me traitor!" roared Gobber. "Do you think I find it any easier than you, you *shrimp*, that the world has changed around me? But that world has already vanished, and the choice we have to make now is between Hiccup and Alvin, who even you must be able to see is the essence of evil!"

"Thank you very much," said Alvin, gratified.

"We may be prisoners of war," bellowed Gobber, "but we can still turn our backs on you, Snotlout! Dragonmarkers! I invite you all to turn your backs on this dog, this turncoat, whose name shall be passed down forever as another word for treachery and deceit!" Inside his cage, the old Warrior turned his back, and all around him, the captured Dragonmarkers, Mogadon the Meathead and his son Thuggory... Grabbit the Grim...Sporta...Harriettahorse—they did the same.

"You can't see me in my box," said Camicazi. "But *I* am turning my back as well."

Snotlout's eyes were feverishly bright. He pretended, with his usual bravado, that he really did not care about his old teacher and comrades turning their backs on him, that it didn't bother him in the least.

"Well, I would be more upset by you turning your backs on me," sneered Snotlout, "if it weren't for the fact that you are the same people who have chosen Hiccup as your leader. I mean, just *look* at him..."

The Dragonmarkers who had turned their backs looked over their shoulders a little thoughtfully at Hiccup, and some of them were suddenly gripped by doubt. Hiccup was a particularly pathetic sight at that moment, half white, half purple, his left hand dragging like a bird with a broken wing, his arm flopping at his side as if it were stuffed with rags, his helmet loose on his head.

"And *Hiccup* is so stupid," sneered Snotlout, "he has even brought the last Lost Thing with him..."

Hiccup was a particularly pathetic sight at that moment.

Almost unable to believe his luck, Alvin reached inside Hiccup's waistcoat with his hook and drew out a struggling, furious, wriggling, coatless little Toothless.

Hiccup looked at the floor, not quite able to bear seeing the gaze of his followers turning from belief to disappointment.

"L-L-LET Toothless go!" squealed Toothless. "I told my mean Master this was a v-v-very bad idea!"

"Oh," gasped the witch in ecstasy, "oh this is too good to be true. The last Lost Thing as well…"

Gobber and the Dragonmarkers gasped in horror.

Their last hope…gone.

"*This time* we will keep good care of the last Lost Thing"—the witch grinned—"and hide it immediately with the others. Snotlout, you have excelled yourself!"

Snotlout bowed low before the witch and Alvin.

"Will you do me the honor of

entrusting me to carry the last Lost Thing to the hiding place where you keep the other Lost Things?" said Snotlout.

His voice was light, casual.

The witch's eyes narrowed.

"That is a very great secret. Nobody knows where we have hidden those things."

"I have proved my loyalty to you both by betraying my former Tribe and kinsmen," said Snotlout. "I am now no longer a Hooligan, but Alvin's loyal subject, an Alvinsman of the Wilderwest."

The witch thought awhile, regarding the boy in front of her with her acute serpent eyes, and then she hissed softly, "We are of course full of gratitude to you for your services to Alvin and to the Wilderwest, Snotlout, and you shall receive your just reward.

"*However…*"

The witch stood in front of Snotlout, her eyes glittering with malice.

"I am not sure that I am going to entrust you with that secret…" she sneered, and every word was like the thrust of a thin, sharp knife. "You have brought me the Hiccup boy, the toothless dragon, sure enough. But do you think that means that I will trust you with the location of the Lost Things? You are a

*Snotlout had turned to the Dark side…*

turncoat, a weasel. You make a good minion, and you are irrevocably bound to our side now that you have betrayed your own forever.

"They would never take you back. No, you are ours now, Snotlout, ours forever."

Snotlout flinched, as if realizing for the first time what being the witch and Alvin's forever really meant.

"And you will have your little place in our new Kingdom," continued the witch. "But I do not trust a weasel, no. For I can see into the weasel's mind."

Now the witch's voice was honey-sweet, and that was always when she was being the most vicious.

"You might be planning to steal those things, in a bid to become King yourself. You know, in your heart of hearts, that you are not good enough, but against all evidence you might have hoped, you poor boy…"

Something in Snotlout's face, a twitch of his mouth perhaps, betrayed that the witch might be right. But proud as he was, Snotlout said nothing.

"You might have thought to trick us all. But"— and now the witch's voice hardened— "Fate knows her business, and she has always only picked two players as possible Kings: Alvin or Hiccup. You were never good enough, for all your fine Viking qualities." Sarcasm dripped from her voice, and Snotlout flinched. "Fate has shown you what you really are, and what you really are is a treacherous worm."

There was a dreadful solemn silence in the hall, as if everyone was witnessing a bloodless death.

If you could kill a person with words, stab him with the pure shock of your spite—why, that witch was the person to do it.

Snotlout looked as if he was about to throw up.

Even the Alvinsmen were gazing at him with contempt.

Nobody likes a traitor.

Snotlout opened his mouth to speak.

No words came out, and he closed it again.

He bowed his head, and his shoulders sagged, and he made himself take up as little space as possible, as if he wished for invisibility. He stepped back into the shadows.

Having thus dispatched Snotlout, the witch passed the

cage containing Toothless to Very Vicious the Visithug, to whom she whispered the secret hiding place of the Lost Things. The implication was clear. Very Vicious was not as clever as Snotlout, but he was a lot more trustworthy.

Toothless's wailing cry was unbearable.

Hiccup could not look at him. He felt like *he* was the traitor, and he had betrayed Toothless.

*ALL MY FAULT*, thought Hiccup. *ALL MY FAULT.*

Inside the cage, Toothless's spines were drooping pathetically.

"M-m-master! Don't let them take me! *Please* don't let them take me! Toothless is *yours*...and I'm the b-b-best Lost Thing..."

"Trust me, Toothless! It will be fine...I'll rescue you, Toothless! Don't worry, it's all part of Plan B!" Hiccup called after him in Dragonese, so that no one else could understand.

But he couldn't be sure that Toothless heard, as Very Vicious had already hurried out the door.

"Now we have *all* the Lost Things!" the witch cried to the captured Dragonmarkers. "Your cause is hopeless! As soon as we turn up on the beach tomorrow, Alvin will be accepted as the new King! It is not too late to repent and turn to Alvin's side!"

"WE STILL STAND BY HICCUP!" roared Gobber the Belch.

The Dragonmarkers yelled their defiance, some more certain than others.

"HIC-CUP! HIC-CUP!"

"HICCUP FOREVER!"

"That's very loyal of you," purred the witch between gritted teeth, "very loyal indeed to stand by Hiccup. But the question is, will the boy stand by you? CHAIN THE BOY UP!"

M-m-master! Don't let them take me!

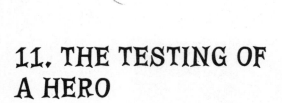

# 11. THE TESTING OF A HERO

Rough hands wound chains around Hiccup until he was trussed up like a chicken.

"Mother, what are you doing?" Alvin said uneasily through his mask. "What did I tell you last time? I have been dealing with this kid for quite a while and the only thing to do with him is to kill him the second we have him in our hook! We have all the things now. We should just kill him, and then we should kill all his Dragonmarker followers."

"We can't go around killing everybody, Alvin sweetest," said the witch piously, "for if we did, we'd have no subjects left. We need to change the minds of his followers, turn them into Alvinsmen, and then we won't have to kill them. It's politics, Alvin darling. Leave the politics to me. OPEN UP THE TRAPDOOR!"

CREEEAKKKKKK!

A huge trapdoor opened in the middle of the room, directly onto the sea below.

"Hiccup is going to break the loyalty of these irritating followers of his by telling us where Stoick and Valhallarama and the rest of the Dragonmarkers are hiding," said the witch.

Stoick and Valhallarama's secret underground hideout was at Coral Beach, the other side of Wrecker's Bay. But neither the witch nor the dragon Furious had discovered this yet.

"I most certainly am not," said Hiccup, as strongly and as defiantly as he could, given that he was almost paralyzed with fear.

"I can assure you, you most certainly are," said the witch. "*You* are going to tell me where your mother and the rest of the Dragonmarkers are hiding, or else I am going to lower you down into this freezing water, wrapped in chains, and leave you down there until you see sense, or you drown, whichever is the sooner."

"I will *never* betray my friends," said Hiccup, really, really hoping that this was true.

"You heard him, he said NEVER!" said Alvin.

"*Never* is a long word," replied the witch. "The Winterfleshers have gathered, so Hiccup will not only have freezing water to contend with, but also the bite of Winterfleshers. Winterfleshers are small, but they are deadly in packs, and they will certainly attack a chained child."

Winterfleshers were small but unpleasant dragons, a little like piranhas. When they attacked in shoals, they could strip a deer down to its skeleton in precisely three minutes.

"SHAME ON YOU!" cried Gobber.

The Dragonmarkers howled their disapproval and horror.

"But he might get away!" warned the strangled voice of Alvin through the mask.

"The Winterfleshers shall bite away at your limbs until you are ALMOST as pretty as I am myself..."

"Pish posh," purred the witch. "You worry too much, Alvin, my little lobster pot. He's completely wrapped in chains! How can he possibly get away? The boy is not superhuman! He's not even a Hero! He's just a perfectly ordinary small boy. You will realize this when he betrays his own people, and you Dragonmarkers will see that your so-called leader is not worthy of your loyalty...

*Oh please, Thor... Don't let me give in.*

"LOWER HIM THROUGH THE TRAPDOOR!" screamed the witch. "AND, EVERYBODY, FEEL ABSOLUTELY FREE TO CHANGE SIDES AT ANY MOMENT!"

The witch's plan was very simple. To lower Hiccup down into the icy freezing water of the bay, water so mind-numbingly cold that it entered the very soul and rendered it dead as an iceberg.

She would dip Hiccup in that water, like a sword smith quenches a sword. Would it make Hiccup, or

**178**

break Hiccup?

Hiccup did not know.

He looked down into the grim, soulless water, and he was shaking already. He had fallen into the sea in winter before, and he knew how it almost burned you at first, and how quickly you turned numb, as if you had ceased to exist.

He also knew what a surprisingly short time it took to die in the winter sea—two, three minutes, perhaps?

*Please don't let me give in...* thought Hiccup to himself. *Please let me be braver than I think I am...*

Down.

Down.

Down.

Hiccup was lowered, by two Alvinsmen Warriors, down, down into the cold, cold sea.

DOWn, down, Hiccup was lowered...

snap! snap! SNAP!

Oh, it was so cold.

It tightened around his chest, squeezing all the breath out of him as if he were being crushed in the fist of a Frost Giant— or was it a Fire Giant? At temperatures that low, they are one and the same.

The witch left him under the water a good minute before she brought him up again.

It was a truly terrifying minute for Hiccup, trying to hold his breath in the freezing sea, trying to deal with the panic, when it seemed like he couldn't hold his breath any longer but knew that if he

*It was like being crushed in the fist of a Frost Giant.*

opened his mouth he would not breathe in sweet air but water.

When the witch drew him up, Hiccup was frost-cold and limp, like a doll with all the stuffing taken out of it. But there was not a mark on him.

The witch was puzzled.

"I don't understand…" she hissed. "What about the Winterfleshers? Are there none down there?"

"There seem to be plenty," said Alvin. "But I told you, Mother, he's tricky…very tricky…"

The witch lifted up the visor on Hiccup's helmet.

"Well?" said the witch. "Are you ready to tell me where the Dragonmarkers' hideout is?"

To Hiccup's relief, he found that he had the courage not to tell her after all. He shook his head.

"Put him down again! This time for two minutes!"

"He'll never betray them," said Alvin gloomily.

It seemed that Alvin might be right.

Twice the boy was lowered into the water, and still he would not betray his friends.

"Patience," purred the witch. "One more dunking will do it. I can see it in the boy's eyes. Not even a fully grown adult can take that water more than twice...and he is just a boy."

The third time the Alvinsmen drew the boy out he was a pathetic sight indeed.

The witch lifted the visor. "Well? Will you talk?"

Hiccup was a little woozy. The witch was swimming in front of his eyes, and he was so cold his brain had turned to ice. Every part of him shivered like he had a fever.

He looked inside himself.

Although a part of him was shouting, "Not back down there! Please, I never want to go back there!" the more important bit of him would never give in.

You find things out about yourself in these rather extreme circumstances.

Hiccup could barely stand, and he was as blue-white as if he were already dead...But still he shook his head and would not say where the Dragonmarkers' hideout was.

And still there was not a mark on him.

"What are you doing, you horrible little boy?" snapped the witch, quivering with temper. "Are you using some fancy foreign breathing technique?"

All around the edges of the room, the Dragonmarkers were crying: "HIC-CUP! HIC-CUP! HIC-CUP!"

The admiration had begun to spread, so that even the *Alvinsmen* were beginning to whisper among themselves: "He's very brave, isn't he? He's small and skinny, but he sure is brave..."

For there is nothing that Vikings admire more than bravery, even in boys with arms like matchsticks. And the fact that the Winterfleshers were not touching him was giving Hiccup a supernatural quality that, at that moment, the witch really could have done without.

"How is he doing it?" people whispered quietly to one another. "The Winterfleshers aren't touching him...Why do you think that is?"

"Maybe there aren't any down there!" howled the witch.

But the sea was so *boiling* with Winterfleshers that, at that very moment, one of them jumped right up through the trapdoor and lay flapping, stranded on the wooden floor, before Alvin angrily kicked it back down through the hatch again.

"I think your plan may be backfiring, Mother... You're turning him into even more of a Hero than he was before..."

HIC-CUP! HIC-CUP!

CLAP          CLAP          CLAP

The exasperated witch ground her teeth. She changed tactics.

"In your heart of hearts you do not wish to become King, Hiccup," she cooed. "For you know that whoever *does* become King will have to make the terrible decision to extinguish the dragons forever with the Dragon Jewel…You don't want to bear that guilt, do you, Hiccup? For that guilt is the lot of a King…"

Hiccup's heart nearly failed.

It was his darkest fear that he might have to do that…

"Well," purred the witch, "I can just take the problem off your hands. We will let you and your friends off the hook. We will give you and your Dragonmarkers safe conduct. You can live free in the Archipelago, anywhere you like. Berk, if you want… imagine living a nice, quiet, peaceful life on Berk…"

Hiccup thought longingly of his childhood home. Of the world before all this happened…

"And the dragons…" said Hiccup. "What about the dragons?"

The witch's voice hardened. "It is too late for the dragons. The dragons will die anyway. But you have it in your power to save the lives of all those you love… Don't let them die all THROUGH YOUR FAULT…"

This was the greatest trial of all.

It was far harder than withstanding the cold, the lack of oxygen. For what the witch proposed was so tempting.

Everything had gone very quiet and still. Hiccup could barely hear the hubbub of stamping and applauding Vikings in the background anymore.

He was alone in the quietness of his own mind.

Hiccup looked inside himself.

IT WAS TRUE.
HE DID NOT WANT TO BE KING.

He did not want to be King. He did not want the responsibility of it being all his fault when things went wrong.

But then, his own voice spoke back to him, in the quietness of his brain. If he was not the King, Alvin would be the King. And Hiccup knew what that meant now. That meant the horror of the dragons" extinction. That meant the tyranny of evil dominating the Archipelago and ruling over Tomorrow for this generation and the next. He could not let that happen.

Even though he did not want it, he HAD to be King now. He had to fight for it, not halfheartedly, but with everything he had.

That was the moment Hiccup took on his destiny.

He lifted his drooping head.

"I will NEVER give up fighting you even though it is too late…even though all is lost…even though it is impossible…never never never…"

The witch had failed again.

"I WILL NEVER GIVE UP FIGHTING YOU, WITCH!"

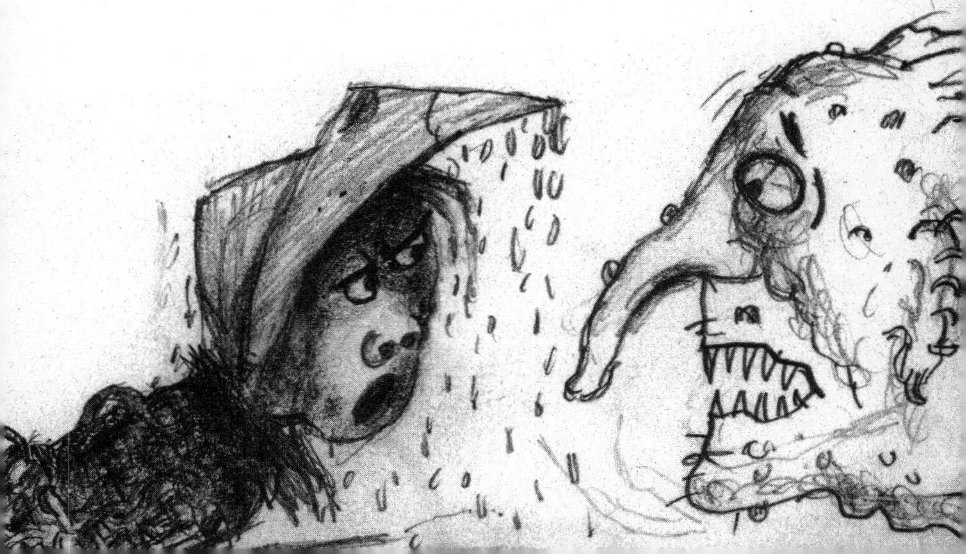

"Leave
him down
even *longer*!" yelled
the witch, quivering with
temper. "Leave him for eight
minutes!"

"Eight minutes is murder!"
bellowed the furious voice of Gobber
the Belch.

But the Alvinsmen lowered Hiccup
into the sea and left him down there for five
minutes, six minutes, eight minutes.

Gobber the Belch feared that Hiccup must be
dead. No ordinary human being could survive

# Leave him down for EIGHT minutes!!

underwater for eight whole minutes. The Vikings held diving competitions in the summertime, so they knew that it was impossible.

But when the Alvinsmen pulled Hiccup up and heaved him out of the water, the boy was absolutely blue, yet he moved inside his chains. He was still alive.

There was a silence of wonder and awed respect in the Great Hall.

The witch pulled up Hiccup's visor with a snap.

This had turned from a trial for Hiccup, to a trial for herself. It was no longer a testing of a single individual, but a duel of their two wills. And Hiccup was winning.

She shook him.

"*Well, you horrible little Hiccup-y brat?* Will you

tell us where the Dragonmarkers' hideout is now, or will I be reluctantly forced to leave you down there forever?

"I am trying my best not to kill you, you ungrateful little so-and-so," grated the witch, "but if you remain so absurdly stubborn, I shall have to go ahead and do that…"

"There is *nothing* you can do to me," panted Hiccup, "that will make me change my mind."

At that the witch's eyes gleamed. "AHA!" she said triumphantly. "Of course! Why didn't I think of this before? *I have been conducting this trial on the wrong person.* We all have our little weaknesses, don't we, Hiccup?" she gloated. "And yours is soft-heartedness. You care more about other people than you do for your runty self. So how about we throw this box containing your dear little Bog-Burglar friend into the water instead of you?"

At last Alvin felt that his mother was thinking along the right lines.

"This is why you will always be weaker than I am, Hiccup," Alvin said. "Camicazi is a very good friend of yours, isn't she? And although she is a great little Escape Artist, even she will not be able to get out of a box wrapped in chains and thrown into the sea.

"She is not a magician, after all."

"TIE A ROPE AROUND THE BOX AND THROW IT IN THE WATER!"

*Stay strong, Hiccup!*

Six burly Alvinsmen threw a rope around the box, with Camicazi's voice shouting, "Stay strong, Hiccup! Don't worry! I can get out of this! Don't betray everyone on account of me!"

SPLASH!

The box went into the water.

"Think of something clever, Hiccup," begged Gobber.

"I will haul up this box, Hiccup," said the witch, very, very patiently, "the minute you tell me where the Dragonmarkers' hideout is. For the last time, will you tell me where it is?"

Silence, while the Dragonmarkers strained forward.

*NO-O-O-O!*

*Don't give in, Hiccup...Don't give in...*
*Don't give in...*
*Please don't give in...*

But Hiccup looked broken.

He nodded. Yes, he would tell her.

Perhaps we all have limits to our endurance.

There was a groan of despair from the Dragonmarkers in the cages.

Their Hero had been found wanting after all.

"It was too hard a test," murmured Gobber forgivingly to himself. "Far too hard a test for one young boy."

"You see..." The witch smiled, faint with relief that at last she had triumphed. "All it took was a little bit of light persuasion...

"YOU SEE!" She glowed, holding wide her victorious arms.

Don't worry! I can get out of this!

"THE BOY IS HUMAN AFTER ALL! JUST A POOR, SQUIGGLY WORM LIKE THE REST OF US!

"Now *talk! Talk! Talk!*" yelled the witch.

It appeared that Hiccup was coughing too much to talk.

"Show me on the map!" yelled the witch. "Show me on the map where the Dragonmarkers' hideout is…"

Hiccup tried to indicate with his head where the hideout was on the map.

"He's too exhausted to talk…Untie his arms from the chains so he can point!" snapped the witch, in a fever of impatience.

"No!" said Alvin.

The witch ignored her son. "Leave the chain around his ankle… Bar the doors…He's only one boy…"

Hiccup's arms and legs were untied.

He stumbled forward, his left-hand side trailing behind him, a dead, unconscious weight.

And then he sprang.

To the witch's astonishment, Hiccup suddenly leaped into awkward, limping life, like a shaking ghost, and used his good right hand to slap the map up into the witch's face. He dodged clumsily past two Alvinsmen, and hauled himself up the Dragonmarkers' cages with one hand, one leg, and a reserve of strength he did not know he had.

"I *knew* it! CATCH HIM!" bellowed Alvin in horror as Hiccup climbed.

"Don't panic!" shrieked the witch. "He can't go anywhere! He's got a chain around his ankle!"

Hiccup hung off the topmost cage, a lopsided scarecrow, his right fist clenched and defiant.

"I will…NEVER…betray my friends, witch! And the dragons must never be destroyed! NEVER! NEVER! NEVER!" shouted Hiccup.

All around the edges of the room, the Dragonmarkers burst out cheering.

"NEVER! NEVER! NEVER! HICCUP! HICCUP! HICCUP!"

The witch gave a shriek of fury. "But we can still kill him! Alvin, you were right! Forget about the politics! Kill them all! Kill everybody! SHOOT! SHOOT YOUR ARROWS! SHOOT HIM DOWN!"

With a cry of delight, Alvin gave the order, drew out his own longbow, ready to shoot…

But he was too late.

Hiccup looked down at Snotlout.

"*I* did not turn my back on you, Snotlout," he said. "Remember that."

And then Hiccup threw himself off the edge of the cage, down through the trapdoor, and into the icy sea below.

"NOOOOOOOOOOOOOOOO!" screamed Alvin, hurling himself at the chain still attached to Hiccup's ankle.

Alvin hauled on the chain, desperate to reel Hiccup in, hand over hook, screaming for help. Three burly Alvinsmen rushed to assist. The chain was coming up easily, for, after all, there was only one skinny young boy on the end of it.

Beside them three more Alvinsmen were hauling up the box that had Camicazi inside it.

"Two more strong drags and we'll have him!" panted Alvin in relief.

The little
blonde
Artist had made
her most
daring escape,

But Camicazi's box came up first—or rather the *remains* of Camicazi's box. The padlocks and chains were broken, the dripping wood was split open wide, smashed to pieces by some great mystery force, and there was no Camicazi inside.

The little blonde Escape Artist had made her most daring escape.

"Noooooooooooo!" howled the witch. "Where has she gone?"

And then the chain that was supposed to have Hiccup on the end of it jerked once, twice...

It was as if Alvin and his Alvinsmen were out in the Open Sea, fishing for mackerel, and the line was suddenly taken by a gigantic shark. The chain was wrenched back with such ferocity that it heaved all four Warriors off their feet and up into the air and dragged them right to the edge of the trapdoor.

"Take the strain!" screamed Alvin hysterically, leaning so far backward that he was practically horizontal to the ground. More and more Alvinsmen joined the end of the chain, heaving for all they were worth.

To the onlookers, it seemed like an almost mystical tug-of-war.

Red, gasping, his masked face bulging, Alvin could not get a grip with his foot and helplessly scrabbling ivory leg. He and his Warriors were towed inexorably nearer and nearer to the open trapdoor.

"PUT YOUR BACKS INTO IT!" screamed the demented villain, and the room watched openmouthed, unable to believe what they were seeing. Who was this boy, to drag so many mighty Warriors across the floor?

"It's a miracle..." breathed an Alvinsman, mightily impressed despite himself, for one of the ancient qualities of a Hero in the Viking Sagas was superhuman strength.

One last colossal heave, and SNAP! The chain broke. All ten of the Alvinsmen fell flat on their backs with a suddenness that dragged Alvin's brand-new cloak into the water, while Alvin screamed, "NOOOOOOOOOOOO!"

Crazed with disappointment, Alvin drew up what was left of the chain. The broken remains were as light as a crabcake. There was nothing on the end.

"AAAARGHHHHHHHHHHHHHHHH!" screamed Alvin.

Killing Hiccup had become his obsession; it filled every waking and dreaming moment. And was the boy to be plucked from his hook in the nick of time once more?

It was too cruel.

The witch's plan had backfired most spectacularly.

"He's escaped! He's escaped!"

"HIC-CUP! HIC-CUP! HIC-CUP!"

"Alvin, my sweetest…Alvin, my darling…Alvin, my honeypot," said the witch, trying to soothe herself as much as her son. "He's dead…He must be dead, don't you see? Some large underwater sea creature must have got him, that is what will have broken that chain…"

"Out! Out to the boats! Search every corner! Launch the Bullguards!" howled Alvin, shaking off the witch's arm and leaping to his feet. "NO MORE TALKING! SHOOT THE BOY ON SIGHT!"

NO-O-O-O-O-O!!!

*Find THE HICCUP BOY!!*

*Find the HiCCup Boy!!*

The witch was quiet for
a second, crouched down low.
And then she exploded into action,
screaming.

"WHAT ARE YOU
WAITING FOR, YOU IDIOTS?
SEARCH HIGH, SEARCH LOW,
SEARCH EVERYWHERE!
FIND THE HICCUP BOY!"

*FIND THE HICCUP BOY!!*

203

# 12. THAT TREASONOUS TRAITOR OF TRAITORS

Alvin rushed out the door in a demented frenzy, followed by the witch and the Alvinsmen with drawn swords.

Leaving the cages with the captured Dragonmarkers openly whispering and then shouting to one another: "What happened? They've got the last Lost Thing? But is Hiccup still alive? Or did he die? That treasonous traitor of traitors Snotface Snotlout betrayed us all…"

That treasonous traitor of traitors, Snotface Snotlout, had not left the room with the others. He was still standing in the shadows. Even if you could have seen his face, you would not have been able to read it.

"Boo!"

"BOOOOOOO!"

The room reverberated with the sound of the shouting, furious Dragonmarkers rattling their cages, and it was dreadful indeed to hear their condemnation.

"TURNCOAT! TRAITOR! LOWEST OF THE LOW! DISGRACE TO YOUR TRIBE!"

There was shame in Snotlout's flushed face as all around him his former companions cursed his name and howled furious contempt.

He would never be trusted again. Not even Alvin and the witch trusted him. He had nowhere to go.

It was a far greater disgrace for a Viking to lose his honor than to lose his beard.

A single tear rolled down Snotlout's cheek.

Once upon a lifetime ago, Snotlout had been Gobber the Belch's favorite pupil. Now it was Gobber the Belch's powerful bellow that reverberated around the room in rolling echoes, like the honk of an outraged walrus.

"YOU HAVE DISHONORED THE NAME OF HOOLIGAN! YOU HAVE SHAMED THE GOOD NAME OF YOUR FATHER AND OF YOUR FATHER'S FATHER'S FATHER! SAGAS WILL BE TOLD OF YOUR IGNOMINY FOREVER!" roared Gobber.

Snotlout stood perfectly still.

And then out loud, he said to himself: "Hiccup knew that I was going to betray him. He *knew*."

Only two Alvinsmen were left in the room. They were kneeling around the trapdoor, peering down into the sea, shivering and with swords drawn, as if that magical Hero, Hiccup the Outcast, might in some final act of superhuman sorcery rise up out of the sea and strike them down.

With a quickness Gobber would have been proud of in the old days, Snotlout walked up behind them, removed the keys from their belts, and shoved them into the water.

The bellows from the cages of the Dragonmarkers died down.

What was the traitor doing? Why had he attacked the Alvinsmen? What in Valhalla was going on?

Snotlout ran to Gobber's cage and put the key in the lock.

"What are you doing, Snotlout, you villain?" cried Thuggory the Meathead in bewilderment.

A single tear rolled down Snotlout's cheek.

"What does it look like, O Dumbo-brain Meathead?" said Snotlout as the door to Gobber's cage swung open. "I'm helping you escape."

There was a murmur of astonishment along the cages.

Vikings were strong Warriors, tough soldiers. But they were not all of them quick on the uptake. They might have been taught spying and treachery in their pirate classes, but most of them, to be honest, were not very good at it. What they *really* liked was to know exactly who their enemies were, preferably color-coded, with the same helmets, or a similar style of furry cloak or something, to avoid confusion in battle.

So this unexpected move on the part of Snotlout really flummoxed them.

"Hang on," said Thuggory the Meathead plaintively. "I thought you were on the other side?"

"Me too," complained Grabbit the Grim. "The witch thanked you and everything…Why are you freeing us? What's going on?"

"Look here, Snotlout," demanded Boily of Bashem. "Let's be absolutely clear. Are you on that rotter Alvin's side or *not*?"

"You won't believe me, whatever I say," replied

Snotlout. "You already told me I'm a double-crossing worm."

Gobber's cage door was still hanging open. But the great giant within, with his arms crossed, refused to move.

"I don't accept help from traitors or disgraces to their Tribe!" roared Gobber furiously.

"Oh for Thor's sake, stay if you want to! You always were a stubborn old warthog," muttered Snotlout. He tossed the keys through the door of the nearest cage so that the others could free themselves, and ran out of the room.

The Dragonmarkers did not waste any further time trying to work out Snotlout's motivation and passed the keys along from cage to cage. Psychology had never been their strong point.

Fighting, however, was their forte.

With cries of joy, the freed Dragonmarkers armed themselves with swords, javelins, spears, whatever they could find in the armory.

Even Gobber realized it might be better to swallow his pride and join the fray. He left his cage, shaking his head in confusion.

●

# 13. MEANWHILE, UNDER THE FLOORBOARDS...

How did Camicazi and Hiccup escape from the box and the rope? Well, it wasn't quite the miracle that the watching Dragonmarkers and Alvinsmen thought it was.

Let us go back to earlier on, under the floorboards of the floating city, where a terrified Hiccup had whispered "Plan B! Plan B!" down to Fishlegs and slammed down the hatch, leaving Fishlegs sitting on the upturned hull of a boat in the darkness with six dragons: the Deadly Shadow, Stormfly, the Hogfly, the Windwalker, the Hurricane, and the Wodensfang.

"Oh for Thor's sake," moaned Fishlegs. "Plan B! Plan B means that the Lost Things aren't there!"

The ears of the Wodensfang were bright purple and quivering as if electric currents were running through them, which was always a sign that terrible peril was near.

"I *told* Hiccup," wheezed the Wodensfang, "I've seen the Lost Things in my dreams. They're underwater somewhere. But I admire Hiccup's courage in trusting Snotlout. It's just a shame..."

Fishlegs swallowed and finished the sentence for him.

"It's just a shame that Snotlout has betrayed him again?"

As if to confirm this, Snotlout's Hurricane dragon took off from the submerged boat and flew off.

"Where's he going?" asked Fishlegs.

And then he answered his own question.

"He must be joining his treacherous master.

"This is fine," said Fishlegs to himself. "I'm on my own here, but it's fine." He was trying not to panic.

His asthma often got worse in times of stress.

Luckily, Deadly Shadows give off a calming hormone in their smoke when they are in an action situation, and breathing in the milky clouds of steam drifting out of the three heads of the gentle giant beneath him gave Fishlegs the strength to remain calm and to focus.

Fishlegs pushed his broken glasses more firmly onto his nose. He did not want to look like a coward in front of his mother's dragon. If his mother could be brave, then so could he.

"Okay," said Fishlegs, making himself think reasonably, "according to Plan B, we now have to surreptitiously rescue Hiccup. But how do we rescue him if we have no idea where he is?"

Two hundred yards away, a hatch opened in the long platform of the ceiling above them, letting a brilliant shaft of light down into the dark sea. The sound of the shouting and the stamping of feet became so loud that Fishlegs shrank behind the Deadly Shadow's back spines, for fear they had been discovered.

"HIC-CUP! HIC-CUP! HIC-CUP!"

And then the witch's voice, clear and loud:

"LOWER HIM THROUGH THE TRAPDOOR!"

Something was dumped through the trapdoor and into the sea. With horror, Fishlegs recognized Hiccup's helmet.

"O…okay…" said Fishlegs. "There he is…That's Hiccup…Let's rescue him…"

The Windwalker had left Fishlegs's side before Fishlegs had even finished speaking, flying toward the spot where Hiccup had been dumped. In two flaps of the dragon's wings, Fishlegs could see from the bubbles that the Windwalker had reached Hiccup underwater, closely followed by the Wodensfang, Stormfly, and the Hogfly.

Fishlegs hovered near the spot on the back of the Deadly Shadow.

"Get him up! What are you guys doing?" he whispered desperately from the shadows. "Why aren't you getting him out of there? There are Winterfleshers down there and everything…"

He could see the quick black silhouettes of the heavily fanged Winterfleshers being chased hither and thither underwater by the hunting dragons.

The Alvinsmen pulled on the chain again. It drew taut, and UP the blue dripping figure of Hiccup was hauled, and Fishlegs watched, openmouthed.

SPLASH!

Up rocketed the Wodensfang out of the water.

"Why didn't you rescue him?" whispered an agitated Fishlegs.

"He didn't want us to," replied the Wodensfang. "He kept on pointing up toward the Great Hall. I think he doesn't want us to rescue him until he can get Camicazi out too."

"Oh thank Thor," breathed Fishlegs. "So Camicazi is alive?"

"We're just trying to keep him warm and alive," continued the Wodensfang, "and scare away the Winterfleshers. The Windwalker is blowing air into him so he doesn't drown."*

SPLASH!

Down Hiccup was thrown again, and Fishlegs could see the large shadow of the Windwalker flying

---

* The Windwalker was acting like a dragon aqualung. Hiccup first describes doing this with Toothless in *Book 2: How to Be a Pirate* when he was stuck in Grimbeard the Ghastly's underground cavern. Hiccup and the Windwalker had practiced this in happier times and warmer waters, when they went diving together for crabs in long-ago summers in Hooligan Harbor.

underwater like a giant ray, sending the little dark slivers of the Winterfleshers shooting off in all directions in alarm. Again and again, Hiccup was hauled back up through the trapdoor, again and again he was thrown into the sea—and each time he was left underwater for longer and longer.

"Oh what shall I do?" Fishlegs whimpered to himself. "This can't be good for him...Plan B was always overambitious...How on earth is Hiccup going to rescue Camicazi when he's all tied up in chains and everything?"

Fishlegs's question was answered when SPLASH! The large box crashed into the water, and this time the Windwalker attacked the box, and to Fishlegs's passionate relief, Camicazi came gasping to the surface. He

THE SEA CouLD not HoLD HeR...

reached out an arm to get her out, and she climbed up behind him on the Deadly Shadow and sat shivering on the dragon's warm back, steaming lightly.

The fifth time, when Hiccup dived through the trapdoor by himself, the Windwalker changed tactics. Camicazi was safe, so it was time to rescue Hiccup now.

The Windwalker got a good grip on Hiccup's collar under the water, like a cat holding a kitten, and hauled with all his strength on the chain attached around Hiccup's ankle, the one that Alvin and the Alvinsmen were holding at the other end.

*That* was the mystical tug-of-war that had so impressed the Alvinsmen and Dragonmarkers in the Great Hall.

With a final HEAVE, the chain broke, and with smooth, powerful strokes of his wings, the Windwalker brought Hiccup, gasping, to the surface and deposited him on the boat beside Camicazi.

"Thank you, Camicazi," gasped Hiccup.

"I told you," said Camicazi, "I would never turn my back on you again."

Hiccup grinned. "Windwalker, Hogfly, Wodensfang, and I will find Toothless and the things…Fishlegs and Camicazi and the others, you cause a diversion…"

He had barely finished the sentence before the Windwalker flew off, carrying Hiccup like a limp doll in his mouth, with the Wodensfang and the Hogfly anxiously following.

"Excellent news!" said Camicazi joyfully. "Apart from burgling and escaping from impossible prisons and possibly surfing on dragonback, DIVERSIONS are a Bog-Burglar's favorite thing!"

She sat on the Deadly Shadow, unpacked her backpack, and put on a large blonde mustache.

"Camicazi," said Fishlegs, "*no one* is going to mistake you for a very small Alvinsman."

Camicazi ignored him.

"Now," she said, holding up a finger, "we're going to have to be a *little* bit careful because I reckon there must be thousands and thousands of Bullguards and Alvinsmen up there…"

*thank you, Camicazi*

"And there are four of us…" bleated Fishlegs.

"Six!" corrected Camicazi optimistically. "Your Deadly Shadow counts as three. Which is why I need my super-dangerous secret weapon. Now, where did I put it?" Camicazi rummaged away at the bottom of her Escape Artist backpack, pulling out ropes and keys and all sorts of extraordinary equipment.

"You have a super-dangerous secret weapon?" Fishlegs clutched at the faint hope of what a "super-dangerous secret weapon" offered.

Ideas of battering rams, and spear launchers, and those gigantic Roman catapults swam into his head, and made him feel a little braver.

But no, it would have been hard to fit a battering ram into that teeny-weeny little backpack.

Camicazi whooped in triumph as she finally located the super-dangerous secret weapon and held it up so that Fishlegs could see it.

There was a short silence.

"Camicazi," said Fishlegs. "The four— no, sorry, *six* of us are about to face Alvin's entire heavily armed army, and that is a small glass jar filled with pebbles."

It was indeed a small glass jar filled with pebbles.

*Ah yes, but these are no ORDINARY pebbles...*

Small, gray, and very normal-looking pebbles.

"Ah yes," said Camicazi craftily, "but these are no *ordinary* pebbles. My mother burgled them off a Chinese ship she raided when she was out east a while back, and I sort of borrowed them. Trust me, Fishlegs, these things are quite something."

"Oh yes," said Fishlegs sarcastically, "those little pebbly souvenirs that your mother got on her holidays are really going to make the difference…"

"Now, we *are* a little outnumbered, I have to admit," said Camicazi, frowning, and pulling out her lassos and her ropes, and borrowing some of Fishlegs's bow and arrows, "so we have to seem like there are more of us. We need to make those rotten, haddock-stinking, twister-evil Alvinsmen think they're

219

being attacked by Valhallarama's whole Dragonmarker army. Can I borrow your helmet a second, Fishlegs?"

Without waiting for an answer, Camicazi whipped it out of his hands.

"Watch this, Fishlegs, I think you're going to like it...

"Who do you think *this* is, then?"

Camicazi sang the Hooligan National Anthem into Fishlegs's helmet, in an uncanny impression of Valhallarama's booming, magnificent tones. The helmet gave her voice the necessary deep, echoing quality:

"*Up with your SWORD and strike at the GALE...*
"*RIDE the rough SEAS for those WAVES
are your HOME...*"

Fishlegs looked at her with his mouth hanging open. "You sound exactly like Valhallarama…"

"Good, isn't it?" Camicazi grinned. "I've been practicing for ages…

*"WINTERS may FREEZE but our HEARTS do not FAIL—"*

"Yes, it's great, Camicazi, absolutely spooky, but this is no time for doing impressions," said Fishlegs, terrified.

Again, Camicazi ignored him. "So, Fishlegs, get out your weapons, put on your hood, and I want you to imagine you're an army…"

"Imagine I'm an army," said Fishlegs, getting out his bow and arrows and pulling up the hood of his Fire-Suit. "Imagine I'm an army…This is crazy…"

Camicazi kicked her heels, and the Deadly Shadow swooped out from under the wooden platform and into the open air of the cavern.

Fishlegs's eyes were shut, and he was whispering over and over again to himself, "I'm an army…I'm an army…I'm an entire super-scary Dragonmarker army…"

Camicazi urged the Deadly Shadow higher and

higher, until it was hovering just below the icy ceiling of the cavern.

Beneath them, the crazy, twisted streets of Alvin's town were curiously beautiful, with flares lighting up the edges of that maze of wooden platforms and the dark shapes of the floating armada.

Little figures were shouting at one another, flares in their hands, peering over the sides of the wooden streets beside the Great Hall, looking into the sea.

"FIND THE HICCUP BOY!" the witch was screaming, and the Bullguards shot out random lightning bolts that formed a hissing, spitting, live maze of death in the air to match the mazy streets below.

"Calmly," whispered Camicazi, keeping the Deadly Shadow circling. "We have to wait for *exactly* the right moment...

"Now *dive!*" ordered Camicazi. "Dive, Deadly Shadow, dive!"

"Hang on!" panicked Fishlegs. "You can't dive now! There's no way you'll get through those random lightning bolts! You can't do it!"

"ATTACK!" ordered Camicazi, more magnificently Valhallarama-ish than ever, shouting into Fishlegs's helmet in Valhallarama's deepest, most commanding voice. Even the mustache had a jaunty Valhallarama effect. "DRAGONMARKERS, ATTACK!"

"Oh brother," whispered Fishlegs, putting his hands over his eyes.

The Deadly Shadow dived.

THE Deadly SHadow dived.

# 14. A LITTLE LESSON FROM CAMICAZI IN CAUSING CHAOS AND CONFUSION

A few minutes earlier, the Alvinsmen had run out onto the platform above the icy sea and scanned the waters below for any sign of Hiccup.

"He won't be able to hold his breath for long!" shrieked Alvin. "Get the Bullguards' searchlights steady on the water!"

Hundreds of hovering Bullguards illuminated the sea around the Great Hall, revealing a heaving mass of Winterfleshers in a feeding frenzy.

"Look, Alvin, my darling! They're eating something!" sang the witch happily. "It must be the boy!"

"I want *evidence*!" shrieked Alvin. "I want a *body*! Anyway, that's not Hiccup. That's my new cloak; it fell off earlier…"

Recently freed by Snotlout, Gobber and the Dragonmarkers peered out the Great Hall door, uncertain whether to attack or escape. There were twenty-two of them, which wasn't really enough to put up a good fight in a straight battle with thousands and thousands of Alvinsmen.

"Wait…" hissed the witch, stiffening as if something had stung her. "What's that?"

From nowhere at all came the disembodied sound of somebody singing the Hooligan National Anthem.

*"Up with your SWORD and strike at the GALE…*
*"RIDE the rough SEAS for those WAVES*
*are your HOME…"*

"I know that voice!" spat the witch. "Surely it can't be…Surely it can't be Valhallarama???"

On the song went, as jolly and as happy and unconcerned as if the singer were singing around the campfire on Berk.

*"WINTERS may FREEZE but our HEARTS*
*do not FAIL…*
*"…HOOLIGAN…HEARTS…FOREVER!"*

Alvin too had frozen. "But…that means the Dragonmarkers have found our war bunker!"

"Impossible!" screeched the witch. "Unbelievable! Inconceivable!"

But the next words were shouted, and to

everyone's ears they were clearly the booming, clear, distinctive tones of VALHALLARAMA the Mighty, Valhallarama the Terrible, Valhallarama the Great and Magnificent Warrior.

"ATTTACCCCKKKKKKKKK!" roared the voice of Valhallarama. "DRAGONMARKERS, ATTAACCKKKKKKKK!"

Down swooped the Deadly Shadow in his invisible dive.

Camicazi must have had the luck of a foolish person, for *how* the Deadly Shadow made it through that complicated mess of Bullguard lightning bolts without being struck was an absolute miracle.

The witch went even whiter than normal.

"Valhallarama's forces..." she whispered. "Quick...Counterattack! Man the barricades!"

Pandemonium ensued, with the Alvinsmen rushing for their weapons and firing randomly in the air as something enormous and invisible swooped down, sank a couple of lightning bolts into the Great Hall, and soared upward again.

Fishlegs opened his eyes shakily.

"Okay, Camicazi, I have to admit, that was kind of brilliant."

"You see"—Camicazi grinned—"we're an army!

We're an entire Dragonmarker army…"

She winked at him cheekily.

"Watch this…"

Camicazi took out a handful of little gray pebbles and flung them in six different directions. They sailed through the air, just normal little gray pebbles…but when they landed…BOOM! BOOM! BOOM! The little pebbles exploded, creating the impression that the town was being attacked in six different places, by six different dragons, all at the same time.

BOOOOOOOOOM!

The sixth pebble caused a very large explosion indeed, as it scored a direct hit on Alvin's armory and hit the blacksmith's fire burning merrily away in the middle.

"HOOOLIGANS FOREVER!" bellowed Camicazi, in what was supposed to be an impression of Stoick the Vast. Even with the help of the helmet, it came out a bit squeaky.

"Your Stoick impression isn't as good as your Valhallarama," advised Fishlegs. "It's about as convincing as your blonde mustache."

Blind panic came over the Alvinsmen.

"They're using Stealth Dragons!" roared Alvin the Treacherous. "Fire randomly in the air because we won't be able to see them coming! They're coming from the air, you fools, the air!"

But it appeared these Dragonmarkers were attacking from the land as well.

"ATTTACCCCCCCCCCCCKKKKKKK!" yelled Gobber the Belch.

And the Dragonmarkers whom Snotlout had released leaped from the Great Hall and began to fight the Alvinsmen.

They were massively outnumbered, of course, but fortunately most of the Alvinsman army had already launched into the air on dragonback to counter an entirely imaginary Stealth Dragon assault.

They shot randomly in the air, mostly hitting Bullguards, who then thought they had been hit by Dragonmarkers and started shooting back.

So began the Battle Underneath the Waterfall, which, thanks to Camicazi's brilliance at causing chaos and confusion, mostly consisted of Alvinsmen and Bullguards fighting one another rather than the enemy.

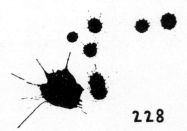

# 15. "YOU RANG, MADAM?"

The Windwalker swam at immense speed through the cavern's inner sea. With intense precision, he broke the surface for a few moments so that Hiccup could take huge, coughing, gasping, relieved breaths.

In the moment that they surfaced, Hiccup heard Camicazi's excellent impression of Valhallarama.

*What is happening?* thought Hiccup, confused and disoriented. *Surely that can't be my mother?*

And then the Windwalker took him underwater again, and Hiccup nearly passed out from the cold and the lack of air.

Beside them swam the little pink Hogfly like an underwater bumblebee, and the Wodensfang.

When at last the Windwalker resurfaced, the floating town was some distance away and they were alongside the Barbarian Armada, quietly rocking in the icy water. The Windwalker gently spat Hiccup onto the nearest ship, and there he lay like a baby, flat on his front, panting on the deck, shivering uncontrollably, too cold to move.

"Thanks, Windwalker..." whispered Hiccup, closing his eyes. He was sleepy...too tired to take this in, and shivering too much.

"Wake up, Master," whispered the Windwalker urgently. "Wake up! You can't sleep now..."

A rush of hot air over Hiccup's shaking body made him open his eyes again. Blinking in the warm breeze, he realized that the Windwalker was blowing hot air over him to warm him. The steamy breath of the dragon gradually heated his shaking limbs into stillness, and Hiccup climbed to his feet, horribly lopsided and as weak as a fawn finding its feet for the first time. His left side was almost completely numb, and even his thoughts seemed sluggish.

He looked back at the Great Hall, now a confused mass of shouting, screaming Alvinsmen Warriors fighting Dragonmarker Warriors and shooting randomly into the air.

Excellent. Fishlegs and Camicazi had gone ahead with their diversion. And it sounded like Hiccup's mother and the Dragonmarker army might have joined them.

The second part of Plan B was going to be a little trickier.

Because the success of the second part of Plan B relied on the Hogfly.

Hiccup looked dubiously at the Hogfly, hovering eagerly before him, spraying Hiccup with water as he shook himself dry.

"Hogfly?" said Hiccup.

"You rang, Madam?" said the Hogfly.

"Hogfly, we really need you now. Everything depends on you."

"Woof, woof!" squeaked the amiable little creature, but he looked anxious. Even the Hogfly seemed to realize that a plan that relied on *him* might be a plan in jeopardy.

"Hogfly, I need you to *fetch*," said Hiccup solemnly.

He reached into his backpack and pulled out the sad remains of Toothless's torn, burned coat. Hiccup had hidden it for precisely this purpose, so the Hogfly could follow Toothless's smell and find out where the Alvinsmen had taken him.

"That," said the Wodensfang admiringly, "is a clever plan, Hiccup."

The coat was sopping wet, of course, and Hiccup had to hope that this wouldn't affect the scent. "Give it a good sniff, Hogfly. I need you to *fetch* Toothless. *Fetch Toothless*, good Hogfly."

The Hogfly gave a sigh of relief. His little piglet tail wagged so fast it was nearly a blur. At last he could be helpful! This was something he understood! This was something he could do!

231

The Hogfly snuffled the
coat all over.

"Hmm..." sneezed
the Hogfly in a deep
little voice. "*Fruity...*"
His sniffer
nose sniffed up and
down, taking in great, woofing
breaths, as if it had a life of its own.

A couple of years ago, Hiccup had taught this
particular Hogfly how to fetch. It had taken a long
time, for Hogflys are not bred for their intelligence.
Their minds hop from subject to subject like
butterflies.

But once they have learned the skill of fetching,
they are, quite simply, the best scent and tracker
dragons in the entire world.

The piggy snout of the Hogfly, snuffling away,
could smell smells that you and I cannot even imagine
smelling. He could smell the shoal of Winterfleshers,
currently passing underneath the boat they were

standing on. He could smell the birds sleeping in the pine trees, way, way in the distance on the faraway shoreline.

His extraordinary little sniffing nose could sort out those smells like an experienced gambler sorting through a deck of cards. And somewhere among those smells, in between the smell of a spider scuttling up the mast of one of the ships one hundred feet away and the twenty-four slightly different smells of the twenty-four slightly different nanodragons currently hibernating in one of the same ship's biscuit barrels, he caught a tiny little whiff of something that smelled a lot like Toothless.

*"Fetch Toothless!"* trumpeted the Hogfly, and zoomed after that smell as if he were being dragged through the air by a Silver Phantom.

The Windwalker and the Wodensfang could barely keep up.

The little speeding Hogfly, like a jet-propelled piglet, flew above the boats that were moored at the edges of this floating city.

Sniff
Sniff

"Fetch Toothless-
fetch Toothlessfetch-
ToothlessfetchToothless...Sorry,
Grandma!" This last remark was addressed
to a ship's mast that the Hogfly dodged in his
single-minded quest. "FetchToothlessfetchToothless-
fetchToothlessfetchToothless..."

There must have been at least a hundred of those
Viking warships, rocking dark and ghostly on the black
water, as lifeless and silent as death boats.

But right at the end, so near the edge of the
cavern that it was right next to the waterfall…were
there dim signs of life? Were there tiny moving

shadows that might have been people, and a
faint flicker of light that could have been the
light of a torch?

The Hogfly was heading straight for
this boat.

*Okay*, thought Hiccup. *So that must be
where the Alvinsmen have taken Toothless…
and if Toothless is there…it will also be where
they have hidden the other nine Lost Things…*

Hiccup had to stop the Hogfly now. The Hogfly
would not understand about being quiet and sneaking
up on this boat. He would give them all away.

Hiccup kicked his heels gently on the
Windwalker's sides. The Windwalker leaped forward
and drew alongside the little speeding Hogfly.

sniff
sniff

The Hogfly was muttering "FetchToothlessfetch-ToothlessfetchToothlessfetchToothless..." to himself with impressive determination.

Hiccup leaned down, grabbed the Hogfly under one arm, and put his hand over the Hogfly's nose. Hiccup's hand got in the way of the smell track the Hogfly was following, and once a Hogfly's concentration was broken it could be easily distracted.

After a few squeals of reproach and "Whoa, that tickles!" the Hogfly forgot about Toothless and licked Hiccup's hand, nuzzling it affectionately.

"Bedtime, now, Hogfly," said Hiccup.

"Ooooh, bedtime! Is it my bedtime?"

"Yes, we're going to bed now, Hogfly..."

Hiccup took off his backpack, and the Hogfly hopped in, wedging his fat little bottom inside and woofing enthusiastically.

"Night, night, Hogfly..." whispered Hiccup. "And well done! You were very useful there..."

Hogflys *love* to be helpful. This Hogfly was so pleased to be praised, he blew himself up into a balloon again, and

236

POP! He burst with pride, even though he had already forgotten what Hiccup was thanking him for.

"Sleep tight!" yawned the Hogfly. "Anchors aweigh! Happy holidays! Good night, sweet ladies, good night..."

The instant Hiccup put the lid on the backpack, deep, snuffling, catarrh-filled snores rumbled from within.

Quiet as shadows, Hiccup and the Windwalker and the Wodensfang flew toward the moving light. They landed on a boat nearby and leaped like cats from deck to deck, keeping well in the shadows.

Suddenly there was a sound of running footsteps. Hiccup and the two dragons dived behind a boathouse to hide. The metal boots of Very Vicious ran past them, hastening back toward the pitched battle taking place around and above the Great Hall, which was now burning as merrily as a gigantic bonfire...

Heart thumping, Hiccup waited until Very Vicious had disappeared.

A ladder rested against one side of the final boat.

Quiet as a ghost, Hiccup climbed that ladder, and peered over the edge.

There were two Alvinsmen guards on deck, talking in whispers to each other. They were so engrossed in their conversation that they did not see Hiccup and the two dragons slip over the side and hide behind the tent-house in the middle of the deck.

The first guard was sucking his finger.

"That wretched little dragon BIT me!" he grumbled. He looked thoroughly harassed. "For a dragon with no teeth, it HURT! If I'd known this job included dragonsitting I'd never have volunteered... That horrible little creature blew a rude raspberry right in my *face*!"

They could only have been talking about Toothless.

"Oh, *well done*, Toothless," breathed the Wodensfang, even though he was normally so keen on teaching the little dragon some manners.

Heart lifting, Hiccup recognized the voice of Toothless

**Toothless was feeling VERY sorry for himself.**

singing to himself, down in the depths of the ship
somewhere.

*Toothless*, thought Hiccup. *Thank goodness you're
all right.*

"One hundred and thirty-three thousand four
hundred and eighty-nine b-b-bottles hanging on
a wall..." sang the little dragon sadly, for Toothless
was feeling very sorry for himself. "One hundred and
thirty-three thousand four hundred and eighty-nine
bottles hanging on a wall...and if ONE green
bottle should accidentally f-f-fall...there'll be one
hundred and thirty-three thousand four hundred and
eighty-*eight* bottles hanging on a wall..."

Toothless had recently learned to count, and
singing this particular song was his way of keeping

his spirits up until Hiccup rescued him. Toothless was convinced, of course, that Hiccup was going to rescue him.

The second Alvinsman had his hands over his ears.

"SHUT UP, you revolting little tone-deaf *frog*! BE QUIET!"

For one moment Toothless stopped. And then he began again, in that same, maddening lugubrious drone:

"One hundred and thirty-three thousand four hundred and eighty-eight bottles h-h-hanging on a wall...one hundred and thirty-three thousand four hundred and eighty-eight bottles h-h-hanging on a wall..."

"Go down and get him to stop!" said the second Alvinsman.

"Why *me*?" begged the first Alvinsman. "He's already bitten me, done the rude raspberry, eaten half my lunch and the end of my favorite scabbard, and we've only had him for five minutes! Why don't you go down and get him to stop?"

"Okay, okay...you have to be firm with these little pests. You're too soft," grumbled the second Alvinsman, and he climbed down a hatch in the middle of the deck. "It's all in your tone of voice. Watch me.

Now look here, you horrible little reptile, pipe down or—*OW! He bit me too!*"

"Don't for Thor's sake spank him!" begged the first Alvinsman. "The witch said he was the last Lost Thing, and it was very important that he was kept in peak physical condition…"

"That's r-r-right, you ignorant Alvinsmen! *Toothless* is the last Lost Thing, and he's the B-B-BEST ONE!" Toothless shouted up from below. "One hundred and thirty-three thousand four hundred and eighty-SEVEN bottles…h-h-hanging on a wall…"

"I'm very tempted to lose him again right now," said the second Alvinsman, climbing up out of the hatch. "He threw up that lunch of yours down my waistcoat and he bit me right on the nose…" The second Alvinsman had never been attractive, but he was even less pretty now with his nose swelling up to twice its normal size.

*Well, you shouldn't go around kidnapping other people's dragons, should you?* thought Hiccup with satisfaction.

BANG! One of Camicazi's pebbles hit something explosive in the distance as the sound of the Hooligan National Anthem rang around the cavern.

"Do you think that's the Dragonmarkers attacking

This Quest is now within our grasp.

us?" said the
first Alvinsman.

"It must
be," replied the second
Alvinsman. "I'd recognize
Valhallarama's singing voice anywhere.
Very Vicious better hurry back with reinforcements. If
we get attacked by Dragonmarkers, we can't defend
the things all on our own..."

The things.

So it was just as Hiccup hoped. They *had* hidden
Toothless with the other Lost Things!

A ship was the obvious place to hide them, so
that if they were attacked they could be carried quickly
to a new hiding place.

*The things must be right here on this ship...*

There was a clatter of feet on the platform behind
them, and a third Alvinsman came climbing up the

ladder, a burly
man with a large yellow
mustache.

"Message from the witch," panted the third
Alvinsman. "You need to get the things ready so that
she can move them to a safer location."

"Are you sure we should get them out of the
hiding place?" said the first Alvinsman. "Was that
exactly what the witch said? You know how cross she
gets if we do things without being told..."

They were terrified of the witch Excellinor. She
had that effect on people.

*Oh please*, begged the watching Hiccup in
his mind. *Please get the things out of their hiding
place...*

"Well, what the witch said exactly was: 'If they
don't get the things out of their hiding place quickly,

I will personally remove their backbones with my fingernails,'" said the third Alvinsman.

This had a ring of truth to it, and the two Alvinsmen began to twist the pulley that hauled up the anchor rope. It took all their strength to turn the pulley around in great, grunting heaves.

And as they drew the anchor rope in, they also drew in the things, one by one.

"Aah..." sighed the Wodensfang in Hiccup's ear. "That was why I kept seeing them floating underwater in my dreams..."

The witch had attached the things, you see, to long ropes tied to the anchor rope. And that was why Snotlout had never found them. He must have hunted through these boats so many times, in the secrecy and darkness of nighttime. But he never thought to look underwater.

She was a very nasty woman, that witch, but you had to admit that she was rather clever at hiding things.

First the Crown came over the side. Then the Roman shield, the arrow-from-the-land-that-does-not-exist, the bracelet that contained the heart's stone, the key-that-opens-all-locks, the ticking-thing (smashed but still ticking), the Dragon Jewel, the second-best sword, and, last of all (and this took a great deal of grunting and straining on the part of the Alvinsmen), the Lost Throne of the Wilderwest…followed by the anchor.

The Throne was covered with seaweed, and as they heaved it over the side, little jewel-like crabs scuttled out of its crevices and scattered all over the deck.

*THE THINGS!* thought Hiccup exultantly as a crab pattered across his foot. *We've found the things! Now all we have to do is steal them…*

"Okay," said the first Alvinsman nervously, "let's stash the things down in the hold so we're ready to move them when the witch gives the order."

The three Alvinsmen hastily untied the things from the anchor rope and carried them down an open hatch.

"Ow!" came the muffled voice of the first Alvinsman. "That horrible little dragon bit me *again*!"

The three Alvinsmen reemerged and the first Alvinsman slammed down the hatch, bolting and padlocking it.

Hiccup drew a little pouch of hazelnuts out

"THE THINGS!"

245

from his pocket. (He always kept little treats for Toothless in his pocket.)

He threw one of the hazelnuts as far as he could onto a neighboring boat and then ducked behind the shadows of the tent-house.

CLANG!

"What was that?" bleated the first Alvinsman.

"You two go and investigate, and *I'll* look after the things..." panted the third Alvinsman. "We're obviously under some sort of attack."

The first and the second Alvinsmen climbed down the ladder onto the next boat, swords drawn, to investigate the noise.

The third Alvinsman was leaning way over the side of the boat, flare held up high, watching them. Hiccup tiptoed up and gave him a big shove.

The third Alvinsman gave a small, muffled scream, and with a satisfying

SPLASH!

landed in the water below and...

CREAK!

Hiccup pushed the ladder down so that there was no way the third Alvinsman could climb back onto the boat again. Then he grabbed the boat hook and pushed off.

*He had the things! He had the things!*

Hiccup's heart was doing a happy little jig.

He hadn't had a great deal of hope for Plan B, but so far, it was working unexpectedly well.

What Hiccup did not realize at the time was that the third Alvinsman was not, in fact, an Alvinsman at all.

It was his own mother, Valhallarama.

You see, Camicazi wasn't the only one who liked to dress up in big blonde mustaches.

Valhallarama had crept into Alvin's war bunker dressed as an Alvinsman, intending to steal the nine Lost Things in time to meet Hiccup back on the beach on Doomsday Eve.

And she would have done it too, if her son had not unfortunately mistaken her for a *real* Alvinsman (the blonde-mustache disguise in her case was rather good, much better than Camicazi's, because she had the acreage to carry it off) and given her a big shove in the back that had thrown her into the water.

"Oh, Hiccup," sighed Valhallarama to herself, as she trod water and "accidentally" let off an arrow in the direction of the second Alvinsman, who was firing at the deck of the departing boat. "I told you not to leave the underground hideout. I *told* you to trust me, and I would take care of everything…"

Valhallarama shook her head forgivingly.

"But then," she mused, "maybe I have to learn to stand back and let the boy do it *his* way, make his own mistakes." She sighed. "It is harder to do that than I thought."

But Hiccup knew nothing of this until much, much later.

He was busy concentrating on the immediate problem before him.

He had to row the boat out of the cavern before those Alvinsmen could raise the alarm. Luckily, the boat was very close to the waterfall. You could hear the roaring of the water, like the bellow of a Seadragonus Giganticus Maximus.

Once he was out of the cavern, he would be fine; the wind would take the sails.

But even though it was such a short distance and not a particularly large boat, how was he to row it all on his own?

Hiccup ran across the deck, toward the oars, and peered swiftly into the hatch just to check that Toothless was in there.

"Toothless?" he whispered.

"Master!" the joyful voice of Toothless squeaked back.

*Oh thank Thor!*

"Don't worry, Toothless!" Hiccup yelled through the hatch. "I haven't got time to unlock this hatch now, but I'm going to save you!"

I have to let the boy make his own mistakes.

"YOU stole my tooth!"

# 16. "MY TOOTH...WHERE IS MY TOOTH?"

And then Hiccup stiffened.

All the hairs on the back of his neck rose like the quills on a fretful porcupine. Not two yards in front of him, hovering in midair, floating in the atmosphere as if they were being dangled by a malevolent god...

...was a pair of evil red eyes.

And out of airy nothing there came a nasty, whining wisp of a whisper: "My tooth...Whe-e-e-ere is my tooth?"

As soon as Hiccup saw those red eyes, he was conscious that his arm had been singing in agony around that horrible tooth for the last hour or so. There had been so much going on he had ignored the pain.

Slowly, slowly, around those evil red eyes with two little slits for pupils, there materialized the body of a Vampire Spydragon, crouching on the hatch as if it was guarding it.

The Vampire Spydragon was a revolting sight, enough to give you nightmares for years.

Its head was that of a gigantic bat, with one huge, cruel-looking vampire tooth protruding from the side of its slobbering mouth.

Its horrible little nose was snuffling as the saliva dripped down its vampire fang.

That pain in Hiccup's arm must have been a sign that the Vampire Spydragon was using the tooth to track him down.

"My tooth..." whined the Vampire Spydragon. "Whe-e-ere is my tooth? For I need to eat what I have bit...Whe-e-ere is my tooth????"

Hiccup said nothing, just backed away in terror, his left arm hidden behind him.

"Aha!" rasped the Vampire Spydragon, its wicked red eyes lighting up in cruel triumph.

"You are trying to hide it, you nasty little burglar, but you cannot conceal it from me...I think I spy it...I think I have found it...You stole my tooth, you horrible little thief..."

"I didn't mean to..." stammered the petrified

Hiccup, taking a couple of steps backward. "You can have it back if you like...I don't want it..."

"You stole my tooth," spat the Vampire Spydragon savagely, "and now that I have found it, I shall finish the meal that I began..."

It crouched for a second, bat wings stretched out. And then it sprang and sank its vampire jaws deep into Hiccup's left arm, exactly where it had bitten him only twenty-four hours earlier.

Hiccup screamed and desperately hit the Vampire Spydragon around its ghastly head. The Windwalker attacked it too, raking at its thick hairy hide.

But the Vampire Spydragon would not let go.

Ironically, Hiccup's whole left side—arm, shoulder, leg, and everything—had just begun to feel slightly better. Now he could feel the paralysis creeping back, a deadening numbness, and as he looked down, he saw the black-purple stain flowering again.

*Vampire Spydragons don't let go*, thought Hiccup. They have jaws like bear traps and they never let go...

Hiccup tried to remember all that he knew about Vampire Spydragons, whether they had any weak points, but his mind was so confused by the pain in his arm he could not remember anything at all.

He desperately punched at the Spydragon's head with his right fist, but the Spydragon merely gripped tighter.

Hiccup was aware that he was screaming, but he couldn't really hear the noise he was making.

What could he use that was around him on the boat?

A confused mess of rope lay on the deck, from where the Alvinsmen had hauled up the Lost Things and the anchor.

Trying to ignore the pain, Hiccup pulled the Spydragon forward so that it stepped into the rope coils, then wriggled and threw himself around in the creature's grip.

Iron jaws still holding tight, the Spydragon thrashed about, trying to keep hold of him, each maddened lunge getting its legs more thoroughly entangled with the rope.

And then came Hiccup's chance.

The Windwalker leaped in and attacked the softer underside of the Spydragon's stomach, which was the rather repellent white of a maggot and provided little defense.

At the same time, the Wodensfang, little old limbs creaking, launched himself at the Vampire Spydragon's head.

The double attack worked.

The Vampire Spydragon screamed in agony and dropped Hiccup for a second, turning to strike at the Windwalker. The Windwalker lunged back and the two dragons locked jaws.

Hiccup limped to the anchor, which was balancing on the side of the boat.

With all the strength he had left, he h-e-e-e-eaved it over the side.

SPLASH!

The anchor landed in the sea below, narrowly missing the head of Valhallarama, still swimming in the water just beside the boat, and swamping her so thoroughly that it removed her blonde mustache.

There was an intervening pause, where the weight of the sinking anchor pulled on the rope, which then whipped around the deck as if it were a live serpent.

The Spydragon shook off the Windwalker, and

turned again to face Hiccup, jaws wide in an avenging scream…Its red eyes fixed on Hiccup. It crouched down to pounce, and this time it would aim for Hiccup's heart. The Death Strike.

But just as it leaped, the whirling, spinning rope of the anchor pulled tight around the Spydragon's leg, and an expression of comical surprise came over the Spydragon's face (if anything that terrifying could ever really look comical) as it was dragged violently across the deck and over the side and into the water, this time with a really resounding…

# SPLASSSHHHH!

Hiccup clasped his hand to his arm, which was bleeding profusely.

Sticking out of the wound was another Vampire Spydragon tooth.

*Now I have a pair!* thought Hiccup, a little hysterically.

He tried to pull it out, but like the first one, it was in too deep. So he tore a strip from his shirt to bind up the wound.

CLAP! CLAP! CLAP!

There was a slow, derisive clapping of hands behind him.

Hiccup straightened and turned around unsteadily…

And there, leaning against the mast of the ship, one leg elegantly crossed over another, was *Snotlout*.

# 17. THE SWORDFIGHT

"Well done, Useless, well done," drawled Snotlout. "Very neat dealing with the Spydragon there. I really thought you were a goner."

The Hurricane sloped out from behind the mast, growling warningly. The Windwalker snarled in response, and the two riding dragons paced warily around each other on the deck, their spines pointing upward as if they were about to fight.

Hiccup caught his breath.

It was impossible to read the expression on Snotlout's face.

"Snotlout…" he said slowly.

"Yes, yes, yes," said Snotlout, waving his hand dismissively. "I know, I'm a villain, and a rogue, and a Very Naughty Boy, and everything, and I betrayed all you goody-goodies, and aren't I terrible, tut tut TUT, but let's get this ship sailing and out of the cavern first, and then we can argue to our hearts' content…"

Hiccup and Snotlout took up an oar each and rowed toward the waterfall.

Soft as a shadow and unnoticed in that lightning-lit cavern with the Battle Underneath the Waterfall raging at its height, the ship carrying the Lost

Things slipped out from under the waterfall and into Wrecker's Bay.

Snotlout put away his oar and took out his sword.

"Fight me," said Snotlout.

"But I don't want to fight you," said Hiccup.

"FIGHT ME!" roared Snotlout.

"I haven't got a sword," said Hiccup.

Snotlout always carried two swords, and he threw Hiccup his second-best one. With the other, he made furious imaginary passes in the air.

"Why don't you want to fight me? Is it because you are scared?"

"Not really," admitted Hiccup, and that seemed to enrage Snotlout even further. "I'm a little scared, but

Fight me to the death.

mostly I just don't want to fight you."

"You *ought* to be scared," said Snotlout. "That bite from the Vampire Spydragon means you won't be able to use your left hand. FIGHT ME! I have betrayed you yet again...*Why* won't you hate me?"

Snotlout was so flushed with anger, in such a state of emotion, that the words came tumbling out as if they were beyond his control. "HATE ME!"

"Snotlout, I don't hate you...and I forgive you for betraying me again. I understand why you keep doing it..."

"Oooh, you are *so* irritating. You keep being so heroic all the time. Stop forgiving me. *Stop it! You don't understand anything!* I DON'T WANT TO BE FORGIVEN!"

"Snotlout, I don't want to fight you, because I think we should be trying to get these Lost Things out of here..."

"But I'm *NOT ON YOUR SIDE*!" howled Snotlout. "*IF YOU WON'T FIGHT ME NOW, I SWEAR I WILL KILL YOU!*"

Hiccup shrugged off his backpack with the sleeping Hogfly in it and put it carefully down in a coil of rope so the little dragon wouldn't get hurt. Hiccup's eyes never left Snotlout's face.

"All right, then,"
said Hiccup, "if you insist."

Snotlout lunged at him.

Automatically (and clumsily, for it was
with his right hand), Hiccup parried the
lunge.

"Oh dear," sighed the Wodensfang,
sadly fluttering down to perch on the tiller.

262

"Some humans…always fighting…if only it didn't have to be this way…"

With a cry of horror, the Windwalker dived down to protect his master…but was attacked in midair by the Hurricane, who brought him rolling down into the sea.

Snotlout slashed forward with a Flashburn Fancy that overwhelmed Hiccup's guard and gave him a nasty gash on the shoulder that stung like a viper's bite.

Hiccup only just managed to throw the larger boy off and roll out of the way, before clumsily ducking behind the masthead. His left side was so numb now it was like dragging a great dead weight.

"All right," screamed Snotlout, beside himself with rage. "Mr. Smarty-Pants, I'm-such-a-Hero, I'm-so-good-at-putting-myself-in-other-people's-shoes, you tell me, Hiccup. You tell me why I keep betraying you all the time!"

He lunged forward, trying to reach Hiccup with his sword around the mast.

"I think it's because you could have been a King yourself," said Hiccup.

This was like adding another log onto a fire.

"YOU BET I COULD HAVE!" screamed Snotlout, attacking Hiccup with every single sword thrust he knew. "*I* SHOULD HAVE BEEN THE HERO! IT SHOULD HAVE BEEN *ME!* I have everything! The physique, the intelligence, the ruthlessness, the charm. *All* I ever wanted was to be a Chief, a leader. IS THAT SO MUCH TO ASK? But it was denied to me, just because I was the son of the second son, not the first.

"Is that not unfair?"

"It is very unfair," admitted Hiccup.

"Until I was three years old, *I* was the Heir to the Hooligan Tribe!" roared Snotlout. "I still remember the respect in everyone's eyes when they looked at me. Their eyes followed my every movement. And you know what, Hiccup? I would have made a great Chief, a grand Chief. Being a Chief would have brought out the best in me...

"And then"—Snotlout's voice darkened—"and then you were born. A weak little mewling mistake of a RUNT...and everything changed..." He spat out each word as if it were bitter as poison. "Suddenly *you* were the center of attention. Suddenly *you* were going to be the next Chief...and then you were going to be the Hero...and then you were going to be the King..."

Snotlout lunged forward, breaking through Hiccup's feeble guard, and Hiccup dodged out of the way in the nick of time.

"Do you want to know why I call you Useless?" yelled Snotlout bitterly. "Because that is what *YOU* made *ME*, just by being born. However hard I try, I will only be the spare and not the Heir.

"*You* made me useless, not needed anymore.

"Before YOU came along I had never been jealous of anyone. YOU brought that out of me. *You* made me pinch you, hit you when no one else was

265

looking…
and then afterward, in
secret, I despised myself for
acting in such an un-Heroic
fashion. Look what you brought
me to!"

"I'm sorry…" said
Hiccup, nearly losing his
footing. "I didn't mean to…"

"And then you release
the dragon Furious from
Berserk…"

"I didn't mean
to…" said Hiccup. "It
was an accident…"

"You *never*
mean to! It's always
an accident! You
take my whole
world from me,
and it's

all just an accident!" said Snotlout savagely.

"There was absolutely nothing wrong with the world that YOU have just wrecked. I loved that world and everything about it. I loved the danger of riding on a dragon's back, the hunting, the storms and the shipwrecks, stealing dragons' eggs from the Dragon Hatching Grounds, swordfighting, bashyball, my whole lost life on the Isle of Berk. I loved absolutely everything about it…

"And then it was gone…"

267

The ache in Snotlout's voice was unbearable. He fought in earnest, with wild, plunging lashes, Hiccup dodging this way and that, handicapped as he was by the weak awkwardness of his right arm and his ridiculous numb leg that made him hop around like a poor broken seabird.

"ALL...YOUR...FAULT..."

As Snotlout pressed the advantage, Hiccup could feel himself tiring. The ache in his left shoulder was becoming unmanageable.

"And then you kept on saving my life, and forgiving me, and it just makes you look like this big Hero, and I'm supposed to be *grateful*...

"Well I'm NOT grateful!

"Because you have taken away everything about my life that is worth living for!"

Snotlout kept ranting between ferocious lunges, either at the gods above or at himself.

"Look, gods, see how good I am!" he shouted.

He plunged forward in a flurry of ferocious lunges.

He made a Flashburn Flunge (a very fancy lunge accompanied by a leap through the air), a Baggybum Balletic (one of his own father's moves, a jump and a stamp, followed by an aggressive launch at the opponent, simultaneously running very quickly past in case you missed them) and five Cunning Remises in a row, as if he were showing those deaf old gods Woden and Thor exactly how wrong they were in not choosing *him* to be the finder of the Lost Things in the first place.

Snotlout's last sword thrust sent Hiccup's own sword spinning out of his hand, and Hiccup's left side gave way beneath him, and he knelt before his cousin, with Snotlout's victorious face right above him.

"Look!" panted Snotlout. "*I AM NOT USELESS! I AM THE BEST! I AM BETTER THAN HICCUP IN EVERY WAY!*"

His face contorted with emotion. Snotlout stood there, the sword pointing at Hiccup's chest, his arm shaking.

"I could kill you now," said Snotlout.

"But even if I kill you now," he raged, "even if I kill you now, and take the things for myself, even if I do that…"

And then he paused, a long time, before he spoke the truth.

"*No one will follow me.*"

"Yes, I'm sorry, Snotlout," said Hiccup, although the words seemed inadequate.

"*HATE ME*, for Thor's sake, you horrible little cousin!" Snotlout shouted. "Why won't you hate me?"

"I am so sorry, Snotlout," said Hiccup, and he really did mean it. "I just genuinely can't hate you..."

"You feel sorry for me, don't you?" said Snotlout fiercely. "You PITY me. Don't you?"

Hiccup said nothing, because they both knew it was true.

"How dare you pity me!" roared Snotlout. "How dare you!

"STOP FORGIVING ME! STOP IT! Why can't you understand? I need to be angry! I have to keep being angry! Because if I slow down and I stop being angry, I have to look at where I am now..."

Snotlout's sword was trembling. Something in his voice changed, from anger to absolute despair.

"If I stop being angry, then I have to look back at what I have been fighting for all these years, and it has all been for nothing.

"If I stop being angry, it bursts on me, like a kind of horror, that perhaps my hatred of you has led me to fight for the wrong side.

"My hatred of you crept in like a green poison and

twisted my judgement, clouded my sight, and led me to
follow Alvin, that evil thing, and there I lost my way.

"Now I have seen what Alvin is and that devil,
his mother, and I know that he is worse than I ever
dreamed evil could be.

"My jealousy has made me destroy all the
things that in my heart of hearts I value..."

"My honor. The respect of
Gobber. The respect of my father.
My whole world, the world of
dragons, dragons that I love.

"If I stop being angry, I
have to see what I am, and
what I am now is what
the witch said. I am a
treacherous worm. I
am worthless, useless,
nothing of value. I am
not surprised that all
those people turned
their backs on me.

"*I* have turned my back on me.

"I have turned my back on myself."

Snotlout dropped his sword to the deck, where it fell on the wood with an ugly clang. He put his face in his elbow. His shoulders heaved with uncontainable sobs.

There was a long and terrible silence.

Hiccup struggled to find the right words, for it was truly awful and piteous to see a person in the miserable state of having turned their back on themselves.

But somehow he found the words of a person who was meant to be a King.

"You are being too hard on yourself, Snotlout," said Hiccup at last. "A weaker person than you would have killed me just now. You could have done that. You won the swordfight. You disarmed me. But you knew that the plight of the world was more important than your own personal feelings. You put your honor before your pride, and that is what Heroes do.

"Do not take this all on yourself. This is not all your fault. Fate and the stars have put us in a difficult situation.

"I know I am not what you wanted in a King," said Hiccup. "I know that it is hard for you to follow someone who is physically weaker than you are and, what is more, your younger cousin. And it is not surprising that it is hard. How can you follow someone who in your heart you do not respect?

"I wish I could offer you a King who is greater than I am. I can't turn into someone else; I can only be me. But I have discovered that I too am stronger than I thought I was. I think I can do this. I think I can be this King who the Dragonmarkers want me to be."

"What are you saying?" said Snotlout.

"I am asking you, once again, whether you will join the Dragonmarker side," said Hiccup.

Another long pause.

Snotlout wasn't expecting this at all.

It took him completely by surprise.

"If you put your faith in me, I will try not to disappoint you," added Hiccup.

"Are you saying," said Snotlout, wonderingly taking his face out of his elbow, "that you are still prepared to take the risk and trust me, after I have betrayed you again and again and again?"

"I know in my heart that you are a Hero in the making," said Hiccup. "We all make mistakes. We all need second chances and even third, fourth, and fifth chances. Maybe you just needed to have that one last fight with me, and then you'd be able to join our side."

Another long, long pause.

It was like a door had suddenly opened in the very dark and tiny room that Snotlout's life had become, a room in which he had been so trapped and cramped and contorted, and he had not seen light for such a very long time that he had almost forgotten light existed.

At last, Snotlout took his face out of his elbow entirely and wiped it with his waistcoat. His face had lost its ill green color, and he looked better than he had in ages.

"You," said Snotlout, "are a very unusual person, Hiccup."

Well, it was better than "You are a little weirdo, Hiccup," which was what Snotlout normally said.

"I haven't really allowed myself to think this until now..." Snotlout said awkwardly, and it was obviously hard for him to get out these words, "but maybe you might not be quite such a disastrous King as I used to think you'd be. You were quite brave back there in the witch's camp, I thought."

"Thank you," said Hiccup.

"And perhaps," said Snotlout, "perhaps Fate does know her business after all. You aren't the King we wanted, but maybe you are the King we need."

He bent down to pick up his sword, slowly, as if he were beginning to recover from a long, long illness.

"I guess I *could* be helpful to you, couldn't I?" said Snotlout thoughtfully. "After all, you would only have one paltry little thing if it wasn't for me. Not much hope of being crowned King with one measly little thing. And now, thanks to me, you have all of them."

"Yes, it's brilliant, Snotlout, I have to say, you've done the most magnificent job," admitted Hiccup. "We'd never have gotten all the things without your help…My parents are going to be so pleased…We're in with a real chance now."

Snotlout drew himself up to his full, dignified height.

He turned to Hiccup and bowed, like a Warrior of old, following the ancient code of the Kings of the Wilderwest, when they invited their greatest Heroes to join them at High Table.

"My sword is at your service, King," said Snotlout to Hiccup.

Hiccup bowed formally back.

"I am honored to accept it," said Hiccup, in the traditional time-honored fashion.

"Shake hands?" said Snotlout, almost shyly.

Hiccup grinned.

Snotlout and Hiccup shook hands.

"Oh that was well done, Hiccup," whispered the Wodensfang admiringly. "You could give that witch a lesson or two in changing hearts and minds."

"Are you all r-r-right up there, Master?" came poor Toothless's terrified voice floating up through the floorboards of the deck. "And wossit he talking about, the one-with-the-nose-so-big-you-could-nest-in-there? Doesn't he know Toothless is the BEST ONE?"

Hiccup knelt down, and he could actually see

Toothless directly below him, through a crack in the deck. He was locked in a cage, poor Toothless, his spines drooping, his eyes large and terrified.

"I'm fine," Hiccup reassured him. "We haven't got time to break into the hold yet. We're just going to sail to a safe place and then we'll get you out of there—I promise, Toothless."

"Toothless not like being t-t-trapped!" squeaked poor Toothless.

"Oh for Thor's sake," said Snotlout wryly, "nothing changes. Stop whispering and blowing kisses to your dragon and help me get this ship out of here."

In all the drama of their swordfight, they had forgotten that they were supposed to be running away.

"Where are we going?" said Hiccup, scrambling to his feet again.

"Across Wrecker's Bay to the Dragonmarkers' hideout," said Snotlout. "I'm presuming you do actually know where that is, after the witch spent so much trouble trying to get the information out of you?"

"The hideout is in Coral Beach," said Hiccup with a grin. "My mother told me that just before we split up in the Amber Slavelands."

"Okay," said Snotlout. "We'll get there just in time for you to sail across to Hero's Gap for Doomsday Eve. You really like to cut it fine, don't you, Hiccup?"

Snotlout rubbed his hands together. He was cheering up in front of Hiccup's very eyes.

"OPERATION MAKE HICCUP KING is on its way!"

"We'll have to be really lucky for this to work," said Hiccup.

"You got any better plans, O Brilliant One?" snorted Snotlout. "Why don't you just concentrate on sailing this boat, and try not to sink it, eh, like you always did with *The Hopeful Puffin*?"

It was as good a plan as any under the circumstances.

# 18. A VERY SHORT CHAPTER IN WHICH IT LOOKS LIKE EVERYTHING IS ABOUT TO GO RIGHT FOR FIVE MINUTES

The boys went to work, getting the ship sailing as fast as possible, expertly handling the ropes like the young Vikings they were. They had done this a thousand times in Viking sailing practice. But never together. They worked in surprising unison, for two boys who had loathed each other all their lives.

Hiccup felt a weird sense of elation for the first time in his life to be working side-by-side with Snotlout for a common aim.

They were not out of danger. No. But, unbelievably, they had all the things, every single one, safely locked in the hold. If they could just get them to Tomorrow…so close now that they could actually see it, a dark shadow in the mist, tantalizingly within reach.

They had finally laid to rest their old quarrel, they had all the things, there was a clear wind taking them across Wrecker's Bay, and for five whole minutes it looked like everything was going to be all right.

It would have been even more inspiring if it

hadn't been for the sound of Toothless howling. Still locked in his cage, Toothless had decided he was going to die, so he had stopped singing the song about the thousands of bottles, and he was now singing an even sadder song, which went something like this:

"Toothless is dy-y-y-ying...Poor Toothless is dy-y-ying..."

"Can't you shut the gummy one up?" said Snotlout through gritted teeth. "It's making me feel like throwing myself off the ship or giving myself up to the witch."

As they slipped out of the witch's harbor, flocks of dragons and seagulls flew screeching overhead, screaming cries of warning, swarming in numbers like a plague of locusts from the direction of the Open Sea.

An extraordinary noise followed them, a noise unlike anything Hiccup had ever heard before, a deep and elemental howl. For one second, Hiccup thought it was the dragon Furious, before realizing that no living creature could make that noise—not even a mighty Sea-Dragon the size of a mountain.

Only a true apocalyptic power could make that noise. Like volcanoes and earthquakes and hurricanes, that noise is one that tells the human being how small and insignificant a pinprick mankind is, for all his cleverness and ingenuity, in the face of the awesome power of Nature itself.

"What is *that*?" shouted Snotlout, his face turning a little green.

"That," said Hiccup swallowing, "is the Winter Wind of Woden."

Just to make their escape a little more interesting than it was already, the Winter Wind of Woden was starting to blow. What were the chances?

Hiccup made some calculations. They might avoid the Winter Wind of Woden if they were fast—and lucky.

Doggedly, quietly, the two boys set the ship in the direction of the Dragonmarkers' hideout and moved out of the harbor, streams of dragons and birds shrieking above them like shooting stars, and the clamor and explosions and fireworks of the battle going on behind them.

So there it was.
Five tantalizing
moments of happiness.

And then...

# 19. EVERYTHING GOES WRONG AGAIN, VERY RAPIDLY

While Hiccup and Snotlout were fighting, everything else had fallen away. They had been so focused on each other and their ancient quarrel that they had forgotten about the peril they were in, their flight from the witch and Alvin.

But now the outside world forced itself on their attention once again.

Just as they got the ship on course, sailing toward the Dragonmarkers' hideout, Snotlout stared with an arrested expression at something back at the waterfall, on the shore they had just left, and nudged Hiccup.

They were halfway across Wrecker's Bay.

Halfway to Coral Beach and safety.

But a little group of black specks had crawled out of the calm, distant waterfall like bluebottles creeping out of a crack in the wall.

Tense with anxiety, Snotlout and Hiccup stared at the distant land, hoping against hope that they were mistaken, that the little black specks were just tricks of

the light
and the wind.

But as the specks flew nearer,
there was a hollow feeling in Hiccup's heart.
He knew what they were.

Ravenhunters.

A flock of the witch's
Ravenhunters, pursuing
them like an inescapable,
unwearying Fate.

Ravenhunters
were too small
for riders,

but they acted as spies for the
witch. On they came, with remorseless
flaps. Flying dragons can easily outpace a ship.

Nearer…nearer…nearer…

"SHOOT THEM!" yelled Snotlout, grabbing
his bow.

The Windwalker and the Hurricane leaped
bravely from the deck of the ship to confront the
Ravenhunters midair as they flew overhead.

Snotlout shot five of them—even Hiccup, with
one dead hand, shot one.

The Windwalker and the Hurricane took out even more, diving after them as the remainder flapped back to the witch, squawking. But there were too many to catch.

"They'll fetch reinforcements," shouted Snotlout. "And this time they will bring Bullguards with riders. Those Bullguards are quick. They'll catch us before we get to the Dragonmarkers' hideout, if it's where you say it is."

It was too cruel.

Even half an hour later, and they might have gotten to safety.

They were so close, SO close to getting away with it, sneaking those things from underneath the very noses of Alvin and the witch...

Hiccup scanned the horizon.

The Winter Wind of Woden, blowing like an angry god, was closer than the Dragonmarkers' hideout.

"Could we steer the ship into the Winter Wind?" asked Hiccup. "They'd never follow us in there."

"There's a reason for that," said Snotlout with a hollow laugh. "It's a guaranteed death sentence. Besides, I don't think there's time. Look! I can see the Bullguards coming out already. They'll reach us before we get to the Wind."

The two boys looked at the Windwalker and the Hurricane.

The things were trapped. They were locked in the hold.

But the boys themselves *did* have a choice.

They could climb onto the riding dragons' backs and fly themselves to safety. Both the Windwalker and the Hurricane were faster than Bullguards.

But that would mean abandoning all of the Lost Things to Alvin and the witch. Including Toothless.

What else could they do? Stay here and die?

"W-w-wossgoingon?" came the voice of Toothless, floating up from the hold of the boat.

"It's okay, Toothless," Hiccup shouted down. "We've just hit a little hitch...nothing to worry about."

The Hurricane gave an unhappy whine, his spines drooping, his tail between his legs. Automatically, Snotlout put out a hand and soothed the Hurricane's splendid, drooping head.

"It'll be all right, boy," he said. "It's all going to be all right."

Snotlout stared into the distance, thinking.

"Oh for Thor's sake," he swore, bending down, picking up his sword, and putting it back in his scabbard. "I can't believe I'm doing this..."

"Swap clothes with me, and give me your helmet!" Snotlout ordered Hiccup, taking off his own helmet and shrugging off his waistcoat.

"Why?" shouted Hiccup, taking off his own waistcoat.

"I don't believe this...I don't believe this..." snorted Snotlout to himself. And then to Hiccup: "They're after YOU, aren't they?"

"Yes," said Hiccup slowly.

"So I'll dress up as you, O Lightning-Brain," said Snotlout. "I'll put on your helmet, and I'll get on your Windwalker, and I'll ride out to meet those Bullguards and their riders, and that'll distract them for a bit..."

"But that's crazy!" spluttered Hiccup. "If you go out there to meet them, all on your own, you'll get yourself killed!"

Snotlout grinned. "Oh, you think my job is crazy? While I'm distracting them, *you* get to steer this ship into the Winter Wind of Woden, and if that isn't crazy, then I don't know what is..."

Snotlout yanked on Hiccup's waistcoat and held out his hand for Hiccup's Fire-Suit.

"Are you sure about this?" whispered Hiccup, putting on Snotlout's helmet.

"Listen," said Snotlout, struggling to fit into Hiccup's Fire-Suit and putting his great galumphing foot through the knee before he got it on, "you're always hogging the limelight, Hiccup, but you know what? It's my turn to be the Hero."

Snotlout laughed out loud.

"I'm on *your* side now, aren't I? I'm a Dragonmarker. We're going to make it out of here with all the Lost Things, and we're going to get you crowned King.

"So the next time I see Gobber," said Snotlout, standing up straight and proud, and speaking in passionate earnest, "he will know that I am a Hero after all. My father will be proud of me. They will *all* be proud of me. They will turn their backs around again and look me in the eye, not with disgust but admiration. The Sagas will sing my name, and they will never forget me."

Hiccup was now wearing Snotlout's helmet and body armor.

As a final touch, Snotlout hung his Black Star around Hiccup's neck.

"There," Snotlout said, with satisfaction. "*X* marks the spot. It looks good on you, Hiccup. It'll give those Guardian Protectors of Tomorrow something to aim at. You are only borrowing this, mind," he warned. "Don't you dare lose it, however scary those Guardians are. Look after it until we meet again. That star is very important to me."

"Hang on, Snotlout," said Hiccup wildly. "You don't have to do this. I'll think of something…"

"But *I've* thought of something," said Snotlout. "You're not the only one who can make plans, Hiccup. Let me do this!"

Hiccup had an appalling premonition of disaster.

"Windwalker! Don't take him!" cried Hiccup.

The Windwalker was an obedient dragon, and in normal circumstances he would have obeyed Hiccup. But the Windwalker had followed enough of what was going on to know that this was their only chance. He gave his master an apologetic, slobbery nuzzle and knelt down so that Snotlout could climb on his back.

"Why you have to have such a mess of a riding dragon, Hiccup, I really do not know," scolded Snotlout. "You're the son of a Chief, for Thor's sake…"

Snotlout reached out and gave the Hurricane a last sweeping pat on one regal, shining side. He rested his head briefly on the Hurricane's flank and whispered, "You're a good dragon, Hurricane."

Before Snotlout climbed onto the Windwalker's back, he remembered something.

"Give me the Dragonmark before I go," he said.

"What do you mean, give you the Dragonmark?" asked Hiccup.

"I don't want to be like that young Grimbeard the Ghastly in the Wodensfang's story," said Snotlout. "Too proud to take the Dragonmark. I'm a Dragonmarker. So give me the Dragonmark."

"How can I give you the Dragonmark?" stammered Hiccup. "You have to have the brand... That long, thin thingamajig that ends in an S."

"Improvise!" said Snotlout impatiently. "You're a King, aren't you? Do your King thing..."

Snotlout knelt in front of his cousin.

Hiccup put his finger in some charred charcoal from a burned bit on one of the masts. Solemnly, he made an S shape on Snotlout's forehead. Then he searched for some suitably Kingly thing to say on such an occasion.

"You are, now and forever, a Companion of the Dragonmark," he said at last.

Snotlout nodded shortly. "Of course, it's only temporary. Until I can get the real thing. But it's important that people know whose side I am on."

Snotlout climbed onto the
Windwalker's back. Hiccup's far-too-big
helmet with the far-too-big plume fitted
Snotlout far better than it had ever fitted
Hiccup.

Snotlout pulled down the
front of the helmet.

Suddenly he looked
like a stranger.

Very noble.

A Hero of old.

Snotlout urged the Windwalker upward with his knees, shouting at the top of his voice, "HEROES LIVE FOREEEEEVERRRRRRRRR!"

# 20. THE LAST SONG OF GRIMBEARD THE GHASTLY

Neighing in terror, the valiant Windwalker leaped into the sky, carrying his helmeted rider toward the oncoming army of Alvinsmen.

For each Bullguard with a rider, there were five more attached to the riders' wrists by long chains, like horses pulling racing chariots in the air. The Bullguards halted, wings humming, not quite sure what to make of a lone boy attacking them. Were there more invisible Deadly Shadow dragons backing him up? *Surely* he could not be alone? Did this impudent human not know how terrifying they were?

Hiccup picked up the backpack with the still sleeping Hogfly in it and put it on his back.

"Don't worry, Toothless!" he called through the locked hatch to his little dragon. "It's all perfectly fine..."

Hiccup turned the ship straight south now, out of the protection of Wrecker's Bay, directing its furling sails toward the screaming hurricane of the Wind.

Farther back and invisible to all, Camicazi and Fishlegs had just left Alvin's underground war bunker and were urging the Deadly Shadow forward. They weren't quite within range of shooting at the Bullguards yet.

"Oh for Thor's sake!" moaned Fishlegs. "That's Hiccup! Why is he riding at Alvin's army?"

The witch herself was seated on a Queen Bullguard, a dragon rather larger than the rest of its species. Her white cloak streamed out behind her. Alvin was on a King Bullguard by her side.

She too thought she recognized Hiccup.

"It's *him*..." she whispered. "The Hiccup boy... his dragon must have saved him...But what is he doing now? Has he turned mad?"

It was typical of Snotlout, somehow, that even in a situation of desperate peril, he was still showing off. For as he flew toward the swarm of hovering Bullguards, Snotlout threw in an entirely unnecessary somersault.

It was one of Flashburn's favorites, a Loop-de-Loop Special, and highly difficult to carry out at the best of times. You had to grip very tightly indeed onto the dragon's back with your knees in order not to fall off when the dragon was upside down.

"You see!" Snotlout called over his shoulder for Hiccup's benefit, though Hiccup could hardly hear him. "I'M THE BEST DRAGON FLYER IN THE WORLD!"

He then tried to get up on his feet, another Flashburn trick, but the Windwalker was flying too fast now for that one, and he hastily reseated himself.

As Snotlout rode straight at the Bullguards, Hiccup could hear him singing Grimbeard's song, the song that Grimbeard sang once, long ago, when he sailed into the west on his ship, *The Endless Journey*, after he had killed his own son and broken up the kingdom of the Wilderwest.

Here is that song that Snotlout sang:

*"I sailed so far to be a King but the time was never right...*
*I lost my way on a stormy past, got wrecked in starless night...*
*But let my heart be wrecked by hurricanes and my ship by stormy weather,*
*I know I am a Hero...and a Hero is...*
*FOREVER!"*

Hiccup could feel the sea beneath the ship picking up more strongly as he sailed closer and closer, nearer and nearer, to that howling hurricane din, the Winter Wind of Woden.

*"In another time, another place, I could have been
a King…
But in my castle's ruined towers the lonely seabirds
sing…
I burned up my Tomorrows, I cannot go
back ever…
But I am still a Hero…and a Hero is…
FOREVER!"*

The Bullguards hovered suspiciously. Their
whiskers were out, feeling the air.

"What is he doing?" hissed the witch suspiciously.
"It could be a trick…"

But Alvin was sensing imminent triumph. He
screwed in his favorite hook.

"No, he knows he's trapped," Alvin gloated.
"That's Grimbeard the Ghastly's Last Song he is
singing there…He knows he is trapped and he is going
down fighting…He is going down like a Hero, trying to
make us look bad, the little rat."

For behind their leaders, Alvin was acutely aware
that the Alvinsmen were whispering to one another,
"Wow, he's still alive…and he's singing that song…."

"ATTACCKKKKKK!" roared Alvin the
Treacherous.

The Bullguards let out a simultaneous scream,

terrible to hear. And the Bullguard and Alvinsman army shot after Snotlout and the Windwalker like a vast swarm of hornets, with the witch still shrieking, "No... *Wait!* It could be a trick! It could be a trick!"

Screaming like a madman with the Windwalker beneath him glazed with terror, Snotlout fled through the sky, pursued by the Alvinsman army.

"Oh for Thor's sake," whispered Hiccup, petrified, scared to look over his shoulder but looking nonetheless. "Oh for Thor's sake..."

On Snotlout charged, howling joyful insults over his shoulder and firing arrows at the pursuing Bullguards.

"Come and get me, you buck-toothed, pig-ugly grandmas! Catch me if you can, you lickspittle, worm-wriggling night-creatures!"

Hiccup was too far away to hear what the insults were, but he almost grinned as he imagined them, for Snotlout had always been brilliant at insults in the Pirate Training Program.

"Take that, you mangy, hippo-slow vipers-for-handbags! Can't catch me, you vile, rabbit-hearted loser-snakes!"

Hiccup was steering the boat very close to the Wind now. Snotlout was sailing very close to the Wind himself, for though the Windwalker could fly much faster than the Bullguards, Snotlout was deliberately flying the dragon slowly to make himself a more tempting lure to chase.

The maddened swarm converged on Snotlout so closely that Hiccup thought for one heart-stopping moment that they might have caught him.

And then Snotlout pulled out an impudent Death Dive, steering the Windwalker down, down, like he was a peregrine falcon diving, at over one hundred and eighty miles per hour, toward the sea.

The Bullguards followed, plunging after him like arrows falling from the sky.

At the absolute last minute, Snotlout brought the Windwalker out of the dive, so late that the Windwalker brushed the tops of the waves with the tips of his wings.

A large number of Bullguards could not correct themselves in time and went plunging into the water. Many others put the brakes on in the nick of time, but were put off course and went spiraling into other Bullguards. When the swarm righted itself, squawking, and set off in pursuit once more, they had lost about a third of their number, who were picking themselves up out of the sea.

"Ha ha! You chocolate-coated pig-dragons! You can't even fly!" jeered the distant Snotlout.

"Okay, now, Snotlout," whispered Hiccup to himself, watching the tiny figure gesticulating rudely on the back of the Windwalker. "I'm nearly there. You need to get yourself to safety…Fly to Coral Beach, and the Dragonmarkers can defend you…"

It was almost as if Snotlout could hear him, for he now crouched down low over the Windwalker's back, and he whispered a word, and Hiccup could see the Windwalker leaping forward.

The only dragon that could have beaten the Windwalker now in a straight speed chase was the Silver Phantom.

He streaked away in the direction of the Coral Beach.

Hiccup heaved a sigh of relief.

And then it happened.

Almost leisurely, one of the Alvinsmen shot an arrow.

It sang through the air…

…and Hiccup saw it clearly. Snotlout was turning, to shout insults or to see how close his pursuers were, and the arrow struck Snotlout full in the chest.

Then
a burst of
flame from
one of the
Bullguards hit him,
and burned through
the safety stirrup, and
Hiccup's poor raggedy
Fire-Suit could not hold
up to the onslaught—the fur
underneath caught fire...the boy
went up like a candle...and fell
from the Windwalker's back.

Down he fell, flaming, like a
falling star...

Down into the cool sea below...

...and Snotlout's light was
quenched.

"NOOOOOOOOOO!"
Hiccup shouted. "NO! NO!
NO! NO! NO! NO!"
The Windwalker gave a shriek of horror.
He was going so fast that by the time he had
wheeled around in a screeching turn and plunged
toward the sea to look for Snotlout, the entire pack of
Bullguards was in his way.

They were no longer pursuing the Windwalker,
for the boy-they-thought-was-Hiccup was the real prey,

and they knew they had killed him. Now they needed the body to prove it to the witch, so the riderless Bullguards were let off their chains so they could dive for the body.

"YEEESSSSSSSSS!" screeched Alvin in victory. "Did you see that, Mother? We've got Hiccup at last! We've GOT HIM!"

"Very clever," hissed the witch. "Well done, my boy…"

The Bullguards screamed too, gloating cackles of victory and triumph and glee most dreadful to listen to. They swarmed, curdling through the sky and diving into the sea, looking for the body of their impudent boy enemy.

So many, many times, when all seemed lost, things had come back from the brink. Hiccup had almost come to believe that he and his friends were invulnerable.

But…

Sometimes time cannot tick backward.

Sometimes you cannot put a dragon back in a forest, nor a witch back in a tree trunk, nor the breath back into a friend when all the breath was gone.

War really does have terrible consequences.

DOWN to the ocean floor, Snotlout sank swiftly, for he was weighed down by his sword and other weapons.

His limbs spread out like a star, he was flying through the sea, falling and ever falling, like soft snow through the air, into another world.

"Heroes who die in battle go straight to Valhalla…" whispered Hiccup.

Snotlout had taken many wrong turns and done many bad things, for he was a boy who had been born out of his time, caught in a world that was changing all around him, and that is always hard.

But it is through our actions that we show who we really are.

In the end Snotlout died nobly, trying to do the right thing in difficult circumstances. And in some ways he would never die, because his name would live on forever.

Hiccup looked down for a moment at the Black Star.

There was no time to think about it now.

His tears were blown away instantly by the wind hitting

him full in the face. He struggled to keep the ship on course.

"I have to get to Tomorrow at all costs...I have to get to Tomorrow...I'll think about it tomorrow."

A cold desperation settled on Hiccup as he pointed the ship ever deeper into the storm.

*Please don't let the Alvinsmen remember the ship.*

High among jubilant Bullguards and Alvinsmen, the witch's white head turned, like the tick of a clock.

"The things...the Lost Things..." she hissed.

Far down in the bay, unsteered by human hand (or so the witch thought), the ship carrying the Lost Things was sailing straight toward the Winter Wind.

"The things!" screeched the witch. "The things! Fetch the boy's body later! We need the things!"

As one, the Bullguard army wheeled around and made like daggers for the little ship, now just a whisper away from the Wind.

"Stop that boat!" screamed the witch. "Stop that boat! If the things go into the Winter Wind, we will not find them again in time!"

"Come ON!" panted Hiccup, drenched to the skin, a little drowned rat in Snotlout's too-big clothes. "PLEASE let me get there…Don't let Snotlout have died for nothing…PLEASE, Woden, great god of the Wild Ride…Let me get there…Let me get there…"

Ah, you know you are in desperate circumstances when your measure of success is casting your boat into the full strength of the Winter Wind.

But as Doomsday Eve loomed, it was the only hope now that Hiccup had of reaching the shores of Tomorrow.

The swarm of Bullguards turned, and the Alvinsmen shot fiery arrows toward the ship. Their arrows lit the sails, which instantly burst into flames.

Hiccup slammed the tiller to the left, swerving to make himself more difficult to catch…The boat shifted wildly underneath him and hit a great wave that slammed her up on her left side.

One of the Alvinsmen generals was riding a Gorebluffer. Gorebluffers swallow large stones, which they can then use as projectiles.

The Gorebluffer swooped heavily

above the little ship, just a whisper away from the Wind, and dropped three large stones the size of cupboards, right on the deck.

CRUUNNNNNNCH!

With a sickening sound of breaking wood, the little ship split in two.

One half, the half containing the Lost Things, sank instantly.

The other, with Hiccup still at the tiller, drifted on toward the Wind.

DOWN the Lost Things fell, down to the ocean floor.

"We got them!" shrieked the witch. "Dive for the Lost Things, Bullguards!"

(Do not fear for Toothless, dear reader. Even though he is inside a cage, Toothless is a dragon, so he has gills and he can breathe underwater just as easily as he can on land. And if the witch gets him—and she may—she will not hurt him, because he is the last Lost Thing. And *he* is the Best One.)

Hiccup had been hit by something, and the cut was bleeding into his eyes, so he could not see. He was barely conscious and mercifully unaware that he had already lost the things.

The half of the boat he was still steering had almost completely sunk, but he hadn't even realized. He was still holding on to the tiller, the lower half of his body submerged in the water.

He was muttering to himself: "Into the Wind… into the Wind…I *have* to get into the Wind…

"Don't worry, Toothless…" he said in his

delirium. "Don't worry...It's fine...I'm going to get us into the Wind...I'll get us there..."

Way in the distance, Camicazi and Fishlegs, seated on the back of the Deadly Shadow, had seen the whole drama unfold, had seen what they thought was Hiccup hit in the chest and fall into the sea, had seen the boat with the Lost Things on it holed just before it went into the Wind and the witch's Bullguards diving in triumph.

"NOOOOOOOOOOOOOOOOOOO!" screamed Fishlegs.

One of the Bullguards had already flown up to give Alvin the key-that-opens-all-locks. It was only a matter of time before they found the other things.

"No..." wept Fishlegs in horror. "It's not possible..."

Camicazi was white.

"No, it isn't possible, Fishlegs," muttered Camicazi. "Hiccup is not dead. I would know it if he were. I KNOW I would know it, if he were...I would feel it in my soul..."

Hiccup was not dead, although neither his friends nor his enemies could see him. He was blindly struggling in the water, hanging on to the sad remnants of the boat.

And then Hiccup was swallowed up by the Winter Wind of Woden. He and his pathetic broken ship were whirled away on the force and rapidity of the tempest, like a tiny piece of bark swept up by a tidal wave.

Hiccup went into the Wind.

# 21. DOOMSDAY EVE ON TOMORROW

During the night, the Winter Wind of Woden wailed like a banshee across Wrecker's Bay and all the way down toward the blasted, cursed island of Tomorrow.

Early the following morning, Doomsday Eve, the witch and Alvin and all their Alvinsmen were gathered on the Singing Sands of the Ferryman's Gift, at the bottom of the Murderous Islands.

A light snow was falling.

The witch had also brought along Gobber and those Dragonmarkers recaptured at the end of the Battle Underneath the Waterfall the previous night.*

The witch wanted them to witness Alvin's triumph before they were executed, so they were standing—sad, chained prisoners of war—at the back of the crowd.

The Alvinsmen were excited but extremely nervous.

Many men and women over the past hundred years had come to the Singing Sands of the Ferryman's Gift carrying false things, hoping, like poor foolish UG the Uglithug, that they might trick the Guardian Protectors into crowning them King of the Wilderwest.

---

*It was a handful of Dragonmarkers versus thousands of Alvinsmen, so the outcome of the battle was not a surprise. Only Camicazi and Fishlegs had got away, on the back of the invisible Deadly Shadow.

All those would-be Kings, along with all of their foolish followers, had died here on this spot, on this very beach.

A place where so many unhappy things have happened in the past seems to retain a memory of that misery. The Singing Sands might have sung once, long before the days of Grimbeard the Ghastly.

But now they sang no more.

Instead a curse seemed to slouch about those shores, as if it were a live thing looking for prey. An overpowering sense of evil hung there like some dense and heavy mist, and even the witch, an evil thing herself, found the shivering terrors ripple through the sparse hairs on her half-bald head as they waited where so many would-be Kings had risked their lives and lost.

"I can see the Ferryman! *Check the things…*" hissed Alvin, his eyes flicking nervously. "We have all ten of them, don't we?"

The witch checked the things once again with a shaking chicken-bone finger. Yes, there were still ten of them, just as there had been when she had looked two minutes earlier.

"Stop fidgeting, Alvin," scolded the witch. "And let's get your Crown straight."

She adjusted the Crown so that it sat more handsomely on Alvin's head.

They had settled the Throne in the middle of the empty beach, and Alvin was sitting on it, adorned with all of the other Lost Things, so he looked splendid—or slightly ridiculous, depending on your point of view.

The witch bit her lip until it bled, for she knew how crucial it was that they got this right. One single mistake meant death for them all. She counted the things one more time,

ve-e-e-ery
slowly, just to
make *absolutely* sure.
"Hmmmff,"
said the sad little voice of
Toothless from his cage, which was
covered with a black cloth to drown out
the noise of his singing. "*You have t-t-trouble
counting to ten. T-t-toothless can count to one hundred
m-m-million.*

318

"One hundred m-m-million bottles h-h-hanging on a wall..." Poor Toothless was just trying to cheer himself up by being cheeky, for he was frightened, and tired.

"Shut up, you horrible little dragon!" hissed the witch, balling her clawed hands into fists. She was absolutely dying to do something dreadful to him, but of course she needed to keep the little toothless dragon safe until Alvin was the King.

The Ferryman was approaching. The waiting Alvinsmen could see a little speck of a boat setting out from the distant shore of Tomorrow, moving through the mist, climbing up and dropping down each white-topped wave toward them, nearer…nearer…NEARER…

But the Ferryman's boat was not the *only* boat in Hero's Gap that day.

As the first rays of morning sun began to rise, they dispersed the mists to reveal the ships of Stoick and the other Dragonmarkers, sailing out from their underground hideout in Coral Beach like enchanted ghosts, and they too were heading toward the Singing Sands.

The witch looked out to sea and licked her wicked gums in glee.

"You're too late!" she gloated. "*Too late*, Stoick, you galumphing idiot. *My Alvin* will be the King now..."

Slowly the Ferryman's boat approached.

"Faster!" screamed the witch, casting a nervous eye toward the approaching Dragonmarker ships. A superstitious part of her still feared that the Dragonmarkers might, in some last-minute battle, take the things.

The witch gave a shriek of joy as the blindfolded Ferryman carefully placed his oars inside the boat, drifted into shore, and came to a stop on the sand.

His sixth sense told this Druid Guardian that he had company on the beach. He climbed out of the boat and strode toward the Alvinsmen waiting on the Singing Sands.

He stopped directly in front of Alvin cowering on the Throne, so close that Alvin had to tip his head up to stare into the Druid Guardian's blindfolded face, which was alarming because of the Guardian's pitiless lack of expression.

The witch was desperate to tell the Druid Guardian to hurry up, for she was worried about those approaching ships of the Dragonmark. But something about the Guardian stopped her from interrupting. It was quite rare for the witch to meet something or somebody who was more frightening than herself. So she bit her bloodied lip and kept quiet, though it nearly killed her to do so.

The Guardian stretched his arms up to the heavens and cried:

"He-or-she-who-would-be-king, approach Tomorrow if you dare!

"Only the one with the King's Lost Things can be crowned the King and live."

The Guardian slowly tipped his head downward to Alvin.

"Are you he-who-would-be-king?" he asked.

Alvin swallowed convulsively. He was regretting having come here at all.

"I am," replied Alvin in a kingly squeak.

"Are you the chosen representative of all the Tribes of the Archipelago?" asked the Druid Guardian.

"HE IS!" yelled the Alvinsmen, drowning out the Dragonmarker prisoners of war, who of course were shouting: "NO!"

"We have a few little dissenters with us," explained the witch nervously.

The Druid Guardian inclined his head. "As long as the candidate is elected by the majority, that is sufficient.

"Have you brought a gift for the Ferryman?" asked the Druid Guardian.

"I have." Alvin gulped.

"Then show me the things," said the Guardian.

There was no change in the Guardian's tone, but something told Alvin that he had perhaps been a little presumptuous to arrive wearing the things, and sitting on the Throne, when he hadn't yet been accepted as the future King.

So with cringing humility and whispered apologies, Alvin took all the things off. He laid them on the beach in front of the Guardian and backed away from the Throne, babbling: "My mother assures me that they are the correct things, Your Worship, and I am taking her word for it, so I hope that if anything by any chance happens to be wrong, or unacceptable in any way, Your Honor will have mercy on me on account of its being an honest mistake, and know that the blame lies firmly at the feet of my mother, who—"

The Guardian turned his blindfolded head toward Alvin just a tiny bit.

"If the gifts are unacceptable," said the Druid Guardian, "the Guardian Protectors of Tomorrow will rise and kill you all."

"Oh…" said Alvin.

Alvin shut up.

One by one, the Druid Guardian ran his fingers over the things.

He passed his hand reverently over the seat of the Throne with its bloodstain, Hiccup the Second's blood, dark brown now with age but still spreading there like a flower.

He took up the smashed ticking-thing. He held it to his ear. It was still ticking: a broken, tiny, valiant tick.

He took the cover off the cage that contained Toothless.

He took a struggling, weeping Toothless out of his cage, and he examined him carefully, even gently putting his finger for a moment into Toothless's mouth to feel his gums. He did not jump or pull away when Toothless bit him hard enough to cause a wound that bled profusely.

"T-T-Toothless not belong to Alvin," wept Toothless. "Toothless is H-H-Hiccup's dragon..."

"It does not matter whom you belong to," said the Guardian, and the witch started, for the Druid Guardian was speaking to the little dragon in Dragonese. "All that matters is who has brought you here.

"Sleep now, little dragon," said the Druid Guardian. Poor Toothless had been so upset and hysterical about being kidnapped that he had not slept at all that night, but when the Guardian spoke in that calm, hypnotic tone, he yawned and fell instantly to sleep, as suggestible as the Hogfly.

The Guardian draped the cloth back over the cage.

The Druid Guardian took a very long time examining the rest of the things.

The witch was so consumed with anxiety that she accidentally bit one of her own fingernails, which was a mistake as they were poisoned, and so they gave her a nasty burn and turned her lips blue.

The Guardian inspected the last thing, the

Dragon Jewel, at painstaking length and with reverent care, before laying it back down on the Throne.

He raised his arms in the air.

The Vikings on the beach leaned in, eyes wide, backs stiffened, in dread of the Druid Guardian's judgment. Unconsciously, Alvin cringed backward, with his hook and arm protecting his face as if expecting to be attacked.

There was a tense pause.

"The things are REAL!" cried the Druid Guardian.

The Guardian's impassive face split with emotion, like a stern stone cliff suddenly struck by an earthquake.

"After ninety-nine years of failure, ninety-nine years of searching, ninety-nine years of guarding the isle of Tomorrow, the things are REAL! The Impossible Task has been completed!"

The Alvinsmen on the beach erupted with excitement.

The witch burst into tears.

She threw herself into Alvin's arms, punching the air with one emaciated skinny fist. "I *knew* it!" she screamed, beside herself with triumph. "I *knew* it!

"Twenty years…" panted the witch, "*twenty years*

imprisoned inside that tree trunk, that little circle of hell. Twenty years I sang my spells, I mixed my poisons, I wove my tapestries of destiny out of rat guts and mice bones. Twenty years of longing, dreaming, and murdering for you to be King…and you will be! *MY ALVIN IS THE KING!*"

"*GUARDIAN PROTECTORS OF TOMORROW!*" called the Guardian in a great, joyful bellow, addressing the Guardians, those dragons-or-something-else lurking beneath the Singing Sands.

"In twenty-four hours, when this King is crowned, we shall be let loose from ninety-nine years of bondage!

We shall be free to roam the skies and seas of the Archipelago, on airy careless wings and feet, with no limit, no boundary, no limitation...

"And I"—and here the Guardian's voice really did crack—"*I* shall be able to take off this bandage that lies across my eyes at last and see the shining colors of this Archipelago, as bright and new as if freshly painted!"

Something extraordinary happened next.

All around the Guardian's outstretched arms, the sand began to sing.

The Alvinsmen were too busy celebrating to notice, and the Dragonmarker prisoners of war too depressed.

But the Singing Sands of the Ferryman's Gift were singing once again.

It was as if each little grain of sand were rubbing against its neighbor, like a million happy crickets singing a joyful hymn of praise.

There was an innocent longing to that sound that brought tears to the eyes.

"At last the Impossible Task has been completed..." cried the Druid Guardian.

"At last our bondage ends...

"At last WE HAVE FOUND OUR HEIR!"

327

"It's going to be *me*!" sang Alvin joyfully as the witch capered by his side. "It's going to be ME! ME ME ME ME! And what an excellent choice that is!"

"He who gathered these things together must be a truly great Hero indeed," said the Druid Guardian. "But wait…I can hear other humans landing on the beach…"

"Wait?" said the witch, instantly terrified. "What do you mean, *wait*? We have all the things, don't we?"

"HOLD ON THERE, MR. DRUID GUARDIAN!"

The Dragonmarker ships had indeed landed on the beaches now. Hiccup's father, Stoick the Vast, great Chief of the Hooligan Tribe, vaulted over the edge of his boat, *The Blue Whale*, and onto the Singing Sands of the Ferryman's Gift.

The Guardian turned as Stoick came running forward, splashing through the shallows. Even in his late middle age, Stoick was an impressive figure, built in traditional Viking chieftain mold, with a belly like a battleship and a beard like a flaming gorse bush.

Stoick was followed by thousands and thousands of Dragonmarkers, including Bertha of the Bog-Burglars; Humungously Hotshot the Hero; his fellow Hero Tantrum O'UGerly and his eleven fiancées;

MY SON

Hiccup is the True King
of the Wilderwest!

Snotlout's father, Baggybum the Beerbelly; and Old
Wrinkly, Hiccup's grandfather.

"WAIT!" cried Stoick the Vast, out of breath.
Running on sand is hard work, particularly once you
have reached a certain age.

"Who are you?" asked the Druid Guardian sternly.

"We are the Dragonmarkers," Stoick puffed. "We represent half of the Tribes of the Archipelago…and this man Alvin must never be our King!"

The arriving Dragonmarkers cheered simultaneously, a great rousing shout from thousands of throats, to show the Guardian how many of them there were.

"It sounds like you have more than a few little dissenters," said the Guardian to Alvin. "If these are half of the Tribes of the Archipelago."

"But they are the *less important* half, Your Honor," replied Alvin.

"We, the Dragonmarkers," puffed Stoick, "have a claim to the Throne. We maintain that my son Hiccup Horrendous Haddock the Third is the true King of the Wilderwest!"

"You have a son called Hiccup?" asked the Druid Guardian with interest.

"*Don't read anything into it!*" howled the witch, forgetting to be polite to the Guardian. "Just because he was called Hiccup, like Grimbeard the Ghastly's son, doesn't mean anything at all!"

"Hiccup actually *found* the things," said Stoick, "every single one of them, and this thief Alvin here and that devil, his mother, *stole* them!"

"Nonsense and cat-nerves!" screeched the witch, spitting like a cobra.

"My wife, Valhallarama, set out to reclaim the stolen things from this horrible pair," explained Stoick, "and she will meet us here, along with Hiccup, whom we put into hiding in case these Alvinsmen killed them. Hiccup should be here any minute, along with the last Lost Thing, the toothless dragon—"

Stoick stopped.

He had been so busy explaining, that he had only just noticed that the things were already sitting there on the beach.

"The things are already here!" said Stoick in astonishment.

"Yes, they are, Stoick." The witch smiled condescendingly. "Well spotted."

Stoick was not the brightest barbarian in the business, so it took a while for this to sink in. His brow furrowed.

"But where is my wife, Valhallarama?"

"Poor, stupid Stoick," the witch said contemptuously. "Always late, always slow on the uptake. We caught your dear wife, Valhallarama, in the act of burglary and revolution in the early hours of this morning, and I very kindly brought her along so she could have the pleasure of witnessing Alvin's triumph before we executed her."

The witch snapped her fingers, and her Alvinsmen staggered over carrying a box on their shoulders. It was the same broken box that Camicazi had been kept in earlier, hastily mended, and wound around untidily with chains, which one of the Alvinsmen unlocked.

Valhallarama exploded out of the box. She was a little crumpled, for a middle-aged woman (even one as fit as Valhallarama) is a little old for being folded up into boxes, but she still had her Warrior dignity intact.

Stoick whitened. He saw for the first time the Dragonmarker prisoners of war standing dejectedly in chains on the edges of the crowd.

"Gobber...my dear fellow, what has happened to your beard? Valhallarama...my love, I don't understand," said Stoick, bewildered. "Have you...have you... *failed*?" he asked wonderingly, for it was unlike Valhallarama, that splendid Hero, to fail at anything.

"Our son did not stay in the underground tree house. He raided the witch and Alvin's war bunker to retrieve the things himself. He did not recognize me in my Alvinsman disguise, and he took the things from me just as I was in the act of reclaiming them," explained Valhallarama.

Stoick beamed. "Oh well done, Hiccup! Very rude and disobedient of him, but after all, if he's going to be a King, he can't have his parents doing everything for him. I'm proud of the boy—" He stopped, and his brow furrowed again, and he said:

"But then...then why are the things here? And where is Hiccup?"

Valhallarama's face was very, very grim.

She turned her face to the witch.

"Perhaps the witch will be able to answer both of those questions," said Valhallarama, and her gaze was as cold and as implacable as iron.

"Yes"—the witch smiled, purring with pleasure— "I can answer both of those questions. I fear you are a little behind the times, Stoick. For you see, us Alvinsmen have ALL the things now."

She whipped the black cloth from Toothless's cage.

Stoick recoiled as if he had been bitten, and the Dragonmarker crowd gave a sigh of distress.

The exhausted little dragon was sleeping inside the cage, a pathetic sight with his wings shivering and dark circles under his eyes from the trauma of separation from Hiccup.

"The Druid Guardian here has just examined all

the things, he has found them to be correct, and he has declared my Alvin to be Grimbeard the Ghastly's Heir. We will be crowning him tomorrow, on the Doomsday of Yule."

"That is true," acknowledged the Druid Guardian.

"NO!" cried Stoick, eyes round with horror.

Howls and moans from the Dragonmarkers.

"But, then…my Hiccup?" said Stoick. "*Where is my Hiccup?*"

The witch gave an infinitely nasty smile. "Your Hiccup is not coming 'any minute.' He will *never* be coming back, I am afraid."

Valhallarama, proud Valhallarama, dropped to her knees. "*No! Hiccup! No!*"

She had never collapsed before. Stoick leaned down to support her.

Old Wrinkly, Hiccup's grandfather, looked thoroughly bewildered. "I don't understand it," he said.

"Your soothsaying was always a little suspect, Wrinkly," sneered the witch rudely.

"It was Snotlout," said Gobber flatly, standing chained at the back of the crowd. "Snotlout betrayed us all."

"Traitor!" cried Grabbit the Grim. Boos and

catcalls from the Dragonmarkers. "That treasonous traitor of traitors!"

Baggybum the Beerbelly, Snotlout's father, put his head into his hands and whispered, "I'm sorry. I'm so sorry. I'm ashamed to be his father."

"So you see how ridiculous it was of you Dragonmarkers to come here trying to steal Alvin's Throne from him!" sneered the witch. "You have nothing—*nothing*! And the Hero you are waiting for is *dead*."

Valhallarama of the White Arms was whiter than a corpse, her hands clasped together.

"I don't believe you," she said.

"I saw the arrow hit him full in the chest myself," said the witch. "But as a precaution we have had our Bullguards and Ravenhunters diving for his body in the bay ever since, so that we can prove that the runt is finally dead. They have not recovered it yet, but what they have found is *this*…"

She produced Hiccup's helmet, like a conjuror, from under her cloak.

"*No*…" begged Valhallarama and Stoick, and Stoick dropped to his knees too.

The two great Warriors knelt together in the sand, as if they were getting married once again, holding the helmet, silent tears creeping down their old Warrior cheeks.

Valhallarama then jumped to her feet and shook her fist fiercely.

"YOU killed him!" she roared at the witch. "You *fiend*!"

"All's fair in love and war, Valhallarama," cooed the witch. "Did you not try to kill my own son, Alvin, with your very own arrow back in the Amber Slavelands? Perhaps you should have given *your* son triple-depth chest armor, and maybe he would be alive today…but then maybe you are more of a careless mother than I am myself. You were never around much, were you?"

The witch had much to pay Valhallarama back for, and that particular poison dart really hit home. The poor, crushed Warrior showed the hurt in her wounded blue eyes.

Valhallarama whirled around, and in one flowing movement, she swiped an axe from an Alvinsman standing behind her.

She raised the axe above her head and roared: "BLOOD FEUD!"

The massed crowds of Dragonmarkers drew their own axes in sympathy. A battle between the Alvinsmen and the Dragonmarkers was about to take place.

Until, with surprising agility and extraordinary strength for one of his age, the Druid Guardian leaped forward, removing Valhallarama's axe from her hand just before she could kill the witch.

He stretched to the height of his full seven feet and spread wide his arms, bellowing in a voice of electric command:

"In the name of Tomorrow, STOP! OR SO HELP ME THOR, I SHALL CALL UPON THE GUARDIAN PROTECTORS OF TOMORROW AND THEY SHALL CARRY YOU UP INTO THE OUTERMOST REACHES OF OBLIVION AND YOU SHALL NEVER SET FOOT ON THIS SWEET EARTH AGAIN!"

A speech that in itself caught attention, even without the Guardian's fingers twitching on the end of his outspread arms, and the sand underneath the warring humans beginning to bubble and sink beneath their feet as if something was happening under there...

Anger turned to fear in an instant.

"Put down your swords!" ordered the Guardian. "This is sacred land! You are quarreling on the Singing Sands of the Ferryman's Gift, and if you are not careful I shall give you a gift that you most certainly haven't asked for and that you will never be able to return!"

Both sides grew quiet, mute with terror at this invocation of the supernatural, and as they did, the Singing Sands fell silent and were still and firm beneath their feet again.

"That is better," said the Guardian.

"I am in command here on these Sands and on Tomorrow. Until such time as the King is crowned, my word is absolute, and if my wishes are disobeyed, my punishment is total. In my capacity as a private individual, I can be very reasonable, but unfortunately my role as Guardian takes me beyond the reach of reason, and I act only as the Law."

Everyone stayed very quiet.

"Madam."

The Guardian turned to Valhallarama.

"I understand the rage and fury of a mother's grief,

but you must put this aside now. The dragon Furious has grown too strong, and the very existence of the Archipelago is at stake."

He did not speak loudly, but he spoke with such authority that it seemed to come from the gods themselves.

"We Vikings are known for our proud independence and our quarrelsome natures. It is the very essence of our beings. But now the dragon has come. We must give up our personal sorrows, our petty blood feuds, and stand together against a common enemy. We can no longer be fighting one another when the future of humanity itself is in peril.

"The dragon rebellion has come! The things have been found!

"The gods have spoken!

"There is a time to submit to Fate and the will of the gods, and the time is now. Madam, put your personal sorrow aside, for the sake of us all."

Valhallarama stood, like a great tree that has been most suddenly struck by lightning, staring at her sword.

"So many years," she said, bringing up her great head, "so many, many lonely years I spent Questing for these things…giving up the warmth of home and husband and my child. What was it all for? A fruitless

Quest. And then it seemed that it all might have been worth it. Sometimes you find that the things you scour the world for are right under your nose at home.

"I thought that there might be a time, when this dreadful war was past, a time for second chances. That I could rebuild my lost relationship with my son, who would have the Kingdom that once I wanted for myself...

"...only for that hope to be taken away from me again. *This man*," she spat in Alvin's direction, "if *this man* is crowned, you will tell him the secret of the Dragon Jewel. And he would use that power to destroy the dragons forever."

"But the dragon Furious would destroy the whole of humanity," replied the Druid Guardian. "Sometimes a King has to do terrible things in order to protect those he has sworn to look after. When the stakes are so high, dreadful decisions have to be taken. It is the responsibility of a King to take on that burden, that guilt, and I know a little about that kind of responsibility.

"Forgive my rough words, Madam. I am not used to speaking with strangers."

The Druid Guardian spoke gently, for he was aware he was talking to a woman who had lost her son.

"There is a time when you have to give yourself up to the will of the gods, and sometimes the will of the gods is a mystery until we see the final pattern in the end…"

Valhallarama tried to square her shoulders. The true sign of a Hero is how they act when all is against them.

Valhallarama nobly giving up her battle glove.

Proudly, she took off her battle glove and gave it to the Druid Guardian.

"I will not swear fealty to this man Alvin," said Valhallarama stiffly. "But I will no longer fight him, either. The Company of the Dragonmark will bear silent witness to the Crowning, if the Guardians of Tomorrow feel that this is the will of the gods."

Stoick the Vast, his head bowed like a broken lion, nodded to give his assent.

"So be it," said the Druid Guardian.

"Hang on a second," spluttered the witch, feeling that the situation, which she thought she had nicely in hand, was suddenly getting out of control again. "This is going to be a private party! My son is the King and these people are traitors and uninvited guests! We don't *want* them at the Crowning!"

The Druid Guardian looked at her thoughtfully. "Your son is not the King *yet*," he said. "And the King must be crowned in front of the united Tribes of the Archipelago, as their chosen representative. Grimbeard was quite clear about that. This lady has given her vow as a Viking that she will put aside her personal sorrow and bear silent witness, and her vow is enough for me.

"She has given her pledge, and now as a sign of your good faith, you must set free these prisoners of yours."

The witch was left with no choice. She gave the order for Gobber and the other prisoners to be released.

The Druid Guardian banged his staff on the beach: once, twice, thrice.

"You have passed the first test. We will not kill you…yet. We will proceed now to the Cursed Lands of Tomorrow, for the coronation of the King. One moment, please, while I address my fellow Guardians…"

The Druid Guardian lifted up his head and arms to the heavens one last time. He spoke with dreadful finality.

"It is the eleventh day of Doomsday, the Heir has been found, and the last chance for any other person to claim the Throne has passed.

"COME, GREAT POWERS OF DEATH AND DARKNESS! Arise and protect the borders of Tomorrow once again! Any man, woman, child or dragon who dares to cross illegally into Tomorrow in the next twenty-four hours will die by the dreadful wrath of THE GUARDIAN PROTECTORS!"

All around the Vikings on the beach, the sand began to bubble, and the land gave birth again to those same ghastly nightmare creatures that had carried UG and his followers to their terrible airy doom a few days earlier. This time, they left the Vikings alone and went shrieking over their heads like shooting stars or asteroids, back to the island of Tomorrow, to guard the borders there.

"What in the name of Woden were they?" Alvin gulped, turning to his mother with a green and sickly face.

"Death by airy oblivion," said the witch grimly. "We were lucky we had the things…"

"The King must be crowned on the stumps of Grimbeard's Throne," continued the Guardian, turning back to the traumatized crowd on the beach as they gazed after those terrifying apparitions. "And the Throne is in the center of Tomorrow. Follow me, all of you, to TOMORROW.

"You may find it harder there than you think."

And as the sun rose higher on Doomsday Eve, the old man in the blindfold rowed his boat slowly, slowly across the Hero's Gap.

He was followed by hundreds and hundreds of boats with tattered sails and burned Vikings, weary and homeless, drained of all hope and energy by this dreadful war.

Far away in the distance, too afraid of Tomorrow to approach any closer, the dragons of the dragon rebellion watched them go and flew to tell their leader.

The dragon Furious stretched out, victorious, in the hot springs and deep snow of his icy stronghold to the north, two trails of smoke leaking from his mighty nostrils.

"They have the things, my lord, all of them…"

said a Razorwing, its eyes dilated with anxiety. "The little gummy toothless dragon, they've got him too.

"And I saw..." The Razorwing was panting with horror. "I saw the Jewel...the Jewel that has the power to destroy dragons forever."

The dragon Furious did not appear to be frightened by this news. "Ah," mused the mighty dragon. "But you see, I have something greater than the Jewel. *I* have the Wodensfang's promise."

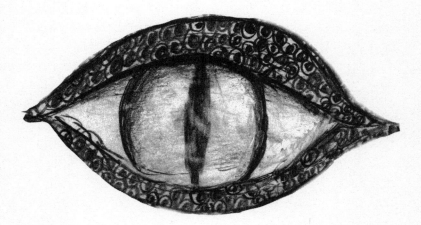

# 22. HERO'S END AT THE ELEVENTH HOUR

Camicazi and Fishlegs had followed the Alvinsmen to the Singing Sands of the Ferryman's Gift, invisibly tracking them on the back of the Deadly Shadow. They had hidden on the sandbanks directly above the beach, and, protected by the overarching wings of the great camouflaged dragon, they watched this whole scene being played out from the safety of their hiding place.

They knew the significance of Hiccup's helmet being recovered by the Bullguards. Fishlegs and Camicazi did not need to hide anymore. They could join up with the other Dragonmarkers now.

Red-eyed, wiping his nose against his sleeve, Fishlegs was about to join the sad procession of boats crossing Hero's Gap toward the isle of Tomorrow when Camicazi stopped him.

"What on earth are you doing, Fishlegs?" she said briskly.

"Um…" said Fishlegs hopelessly, "I'm following the others…There's no point doing anything else, is there, now that we know Hiccup is dead."

"The more I think about it," said Camicazi, "the less I think Hiccup is dead."

"But…but…the helmet…that was Hiccup's helmet…" protested Fishlegs. "And they brought it up from the sea…There isn't really any other explanation."

"Oh for Thor's sake," said Camicazi in exasperation. "Have you not hung around with him long enough to know that you never give up hope until you are presented with an actual Hiccup skeleton, solemnly registered and verified by the Valkyrie Death Committee as completely authentic?"

"Yes, but…"

"We thought *you* were dead back there in the Slavelands, remember, and look! You turned up again large as life—or rather, skinny and asthmatic and eczema-covered as life! What would have happened if we stopped looking for *you*?"

"But…but…but…" spluttered Fishlegs. "But sometimes people really ARE dead, Camicazi! And it's Doomsday Eve…We only have twenty-four hours before the King gets crowned, and Alvin has all the things…

We haven't got a hope..."

"It's a tight deadline," admitted Camicazi. "But then again Hiccup always works best under tight deadlines."

"I want to believe you," said Fishlegs longingly. "I really, really want to believe you, but where IS he, Camicazi?"

Oh DO HURRY UP, Fishlegs!

"OH DO HURRY UP!" shouted Camicazi, already on board the Deadly Shadow. "We'll just have to go and find him..."

"Don't you think you should at least tell your mother we're okay?" asked Fishlegs as he climbed up after her. "I saw Bertha among that Dragonmarker crowd...She might at least want to know you are still alive. And maybe she might not give you permission to go and look for Hiccup?"

"I think," said Camicazi thoughtfully, "it might be better not to ask. You're right, though. It would be nice to let her know that we're alive, so she doesn't worry."

Two minutes
later, Great Chief Bertha of the
Bog-Burglars, solemnly steering *The Big Momma*,
looked up as a great shadow passed above her. She saw
the underside of an enormous three-headed dragon,
briefly turning itself visible as it sailed south in slow,
graceful flaps.

On the dragon's back were the two small figures
of Fishlegs and Camicazi, and Bertha just caught the
words of her daughter, shouted down from the back
of the dragon, before the words were tossed away on
the wind.

"JUST OFF TO FIND HICCUP, MOTHER...
See you later...Don't worry about me! Bog-Burglars
fight forever!"

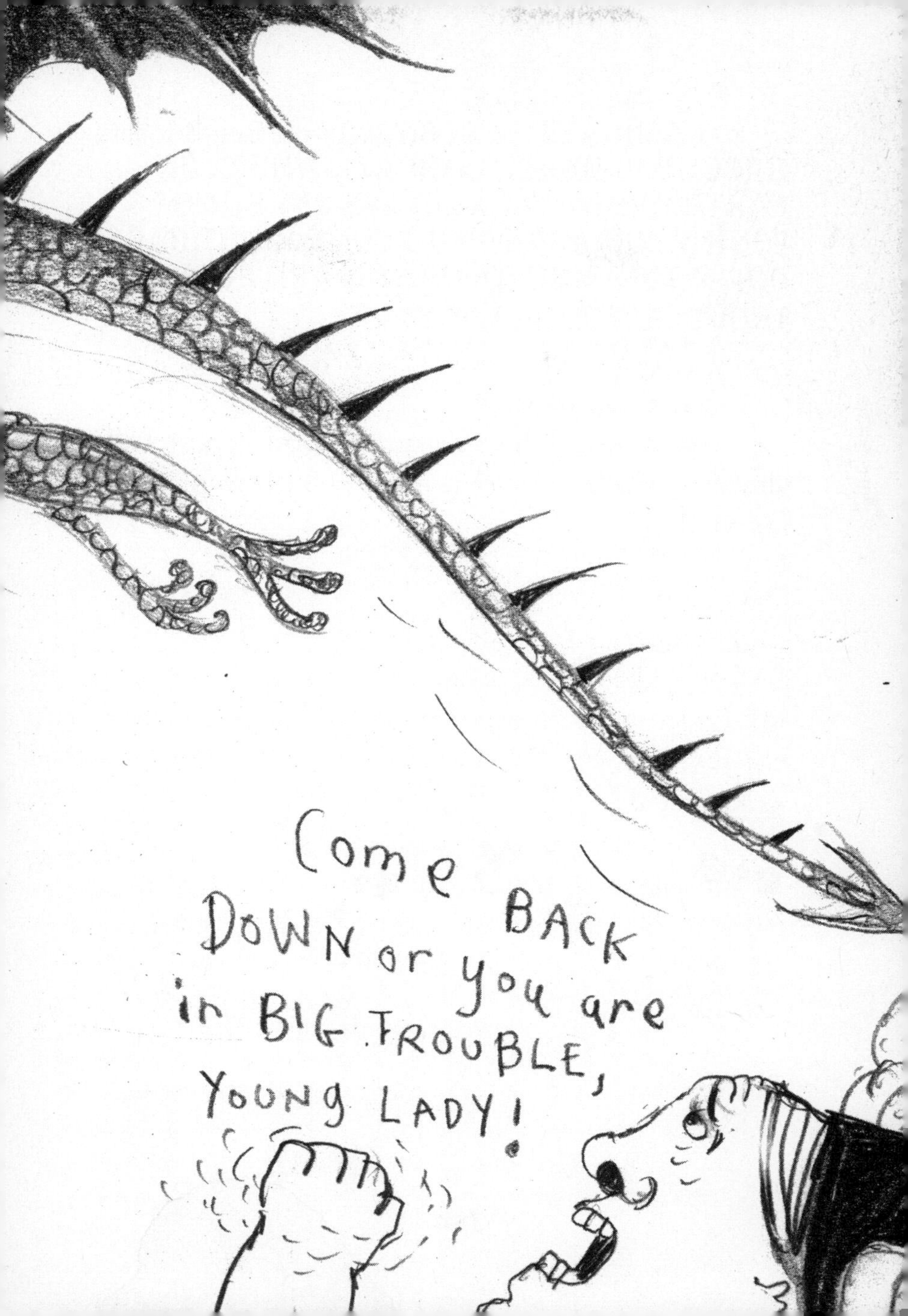
Come BACK DOWN or you are in BIG TROUBLE, YOUNG LADY!

"CAMICAZI!" yelled Bertha of the Bog-Burglars. "HICCUP IS DEAD! CAMICAZI, WHERE ON EARTH ARE YOU GOING? I'VE ONLY JUST FOUND YOU AGAIN! YOU COME RIGHT BACK DOWN THIS MINUTE OR YOU ARE IN BIG TROUBLE, YOUNG LADY!

"CAMICAAAAAAAZZZIIIIIIIIIIII!"

But it was too late.

The beautiful three-headed Shadow Dragon had already slowly faded into invisibility, like breath into the wind.

# 23. ONE MORE DAY

Far away on the little isle of Hero's End, a boy lay stretched out unconscious on a beach.

Camicazi was right.

HICCUP WAS ALIVE.

He only had one day left now.

One day until a King would be crowned on the Doomsday of Yule.

One day to convince the Guardians that HE was the King and not Alvin the Treacherous.

And he had no things. Not a single one.

How would he ever get to Tomorrow?

For the Druid Guardian had closed up the borders of Tomorrow. He had called up his Guardian Protectors to defend the island of Tomorrow from any being, human or dragon, who might dare to try to set foot on the island now that the Heir had been found, and the Crowning of the King was about to commence.

And we have seen just how scary, just how terrifying, those Guardian Protectors can be.

But at least Hiccup was ALIVE. Barely alive, but ALIVE still.

Perched on his chest, his head tucked under his wing with shame, was the little old dragon, the Wodensfang, waiting for the boy to wake up.

I am a TRAITOR,
I cannot see
how this will end
now...

# EPILOGUE

I said, at the beginning of this episode of my memoirs, that the making of a Hero is like the making of a sword.

How the sword and the Hero must be tested time and time again, and the more fearsome and dreadful the test, the stronger the sword and the Hero, in the end.

That boy-who-once-was-me who is lying back there on the beach at Hero's End, he seems to have lost everything, doesn't he?

He risked everything to get the Lost Things, and then at the last minute, they slipped through his fingers.

He does not know this yet, poor boy, as he lies there. He is still dreaming that he is driving the ship with the Lost Things on it, safely through the Wind.

"Don't worry, Toothless," he is muttering to himself, slightly delirious. "It will be all right... Everything will be all right..." Little knowing that poor Toothless has fallen into dark hands and is not all right at all.

It is pathetic, is it not, to see the boy's delusion, lying on that beach like a crumpled piece of driftwood thrown up by the careless gods, as if he were nothing.

But now I am seventy-six years old. Looking back, I have to say that things are not quite as bleak as they seem.

At last, for the first time in the boy's life, he is finally ready.

It may not look like it, as he lies there, broken on the beach, having lost the things, having lost Toothless, having lost everything, but this was the moment the Hero was made.

He is ready to take on his destiny now.

I meet him on Hero's End, hovering over him as he lies there, and I whisper:

*You are ready now.*

*Know this, when you wake.*

*You are finally ready to take on Tomorrow.*

*You may look like a corpse, but you are in fact a King.*

He will need this knowledge when he wakes into painful reality.

For it will be painful.

He will grieve for the loss of the things, and know that it is his fault. He will grieve for Snotlout. He will feel that this is his fault too, even though Snotlout chose to take that risk out of his own free will.

But Snotlout has taught him something.

Hiccup believed in Snotlout. He went on trying

to believe in Snotlout. And in the end Snotlout believed in Hiccup, and that was one of the crucial, final things that gave Hiccup belief in himself.

This was what mattered.

He has carried Snotlout with him ever after. Snotlout and his Black Star are part of his Kingship.

Remember the Wodensfang's wheezy voice, whispering in the darkness of the underground hideout high in the Murderous Mountains, about how a boy can change from being Speedfast to being Grimbeard the Ghastly...

"...*and also the other way around.*"

Back on those ships crossing Hero's Gap on Doomsday Eve, Snotlout's father, Baggybum the Beerbelly, does not yet know that Snotlout has chosen the right side. Gobber and the Dragonmarkers are still cursing Snotlout's name, still believing him to be the most treacherous traitor of traitors, still shaking their heads and their fists, and calling down dreadful imprecations on his head.

But they will find out the truth, in the end.

Time will shake out the truth, as it always does.

Gobber and Baggybum will find out the truth, just as Snotlout knew they would when he hung his Black Star around my neck.

They will know that Snotlout was a Hero
after all...

Gobber and Baggybum will be proud of him
at last.

And long after Kings are forgotten and their
names have fallen into dust, the good deeds and the
actions of the Heroes live on in glory.

Once I dreamed of castles and a crown upon my
head...

Now the night sky is my only roof and the sea my
rocking bed...

But let my heart be wrecked by hurricanes and
my ship by stormy weather.

I know I am a Hero...and a Hero is FOREVER!

As I write, sixty-two years later, I am wearing
Snotlout's Black Star on a chain around my neck, the
Black Star that in the Hooligan Tribe is the highest
honor that can be given for bravery in battle.

It looks a little incongruous on the chest of such
a very old man as myself, but I wear it with such pride,
and it makes me stand a little straighter, even though
I am bowled into a hoop by age and the Archipelago's
howling winds, and I am not as steady on my legs as I
once was.

It is the Black Star that Snotlout gave me when

he exchanged his clothes for my clothes, and his destiny for my destiny. A noble gift, do you not think, in the end, from one cousin to another?

Here is the odd thing though.

Time has rubbed away at the black of the star.

And underneath the black…there was just a glint of something, over the years, and then I rubbed at it, and rubbed at it, until the crusty dark surface crumbled away from the heart of the star, and the star fell out, the metal just as bright and brilliant as when it was first dug from the ground.

Now the star doesn't look black at all.

Just gold.

A HERO…IS…FOREVER.

*Adieu, Snotlout.*

I could not have done this without you.

I carry you with me, every step I take, every decision I make. You are part of my blood, and I would never have gotten this far without you.

We shall meet again, in a better world than this one.

*Even if Hiccup manages to fight those dreadful dragon
Guardians of Tomorrow, the dragon Furious will be
waiting for him.*

# ONE
# MORE
# DAY

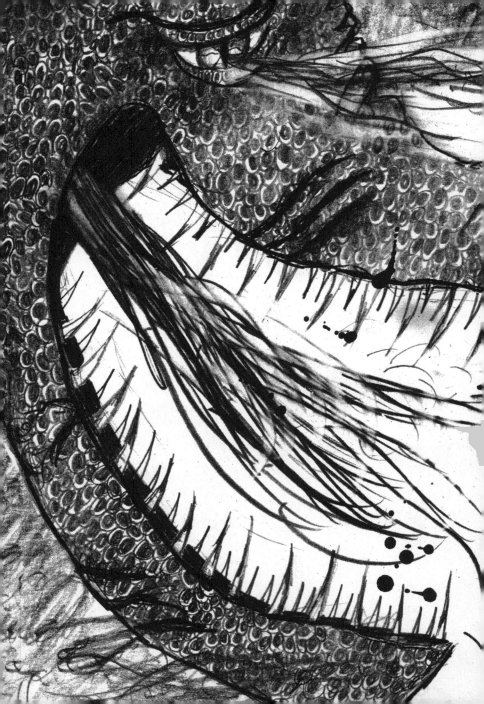

# ONE MORE DAY

*How can Hiccup get to Tomorrow now that the borders
are being guarded by those dreadful dragon protectors who
deal out death by airy oblivion?*

*And how will he get to be the next King of the Wilderwest
now that he has none of the things?*

*Surely Alvin the Treacherous cannot be the King?*

**And surely this cannot be the
END of the dragons?**

*Watch out for Book 12, which really is the FINAL
volume of Hiccup's memoirs.*

"The Dragontime is coming
And only a King can save you now.
The King shall be the
Champion of Champions.

You shall know the King
By the King's Lost Things.
A fang-free dragon, my second-best sword,
My Roman shield,
An arrow-from-the-land-that-does-not-exist,
The heart's stone, the key-that-opens-all-locks,
The ticking-thing, the Throne, the Crown.

And last and best of all the ten,
The Dragon Jewel will save all men."

This is Cressida, age 9, writing on the island.

**Cressida Cowell** grew up in London and on a small, uninhabited island off the west coast of Scotland, where she spent her time writing stories, fishing for things to eat, and exploring the island looking for dragons. She was convinced that there were dragons living on the island and has been fascinated by them ever since.

www.cressidacowell.co.uk

A Hero
is Forever.

Don't miss this full-color guide
to all the dragons!